I0598436

Tears of the Wolf

by

Sharon Buchbinder

Hotel LaBelle, Book 4

This is a work of fiction. Names, characters, places, and incidents are either the product of the author's imagination or are used fictitiously, and any resemblance to actual persons living or dead, business establishments, events, or locales, is entirely coincidental.

Tears of the Wolf

COPYRIGHT © 2020 by Sharon Buchbinder

All rights reserved. No part of this book may be used or reproduced in any manner whatsoever without written permission of the author or The Wild Rose Press, Inc. except in the case of brief quotations embodied in critical articles or reviews.
Contact Information: info@thewildrosepress.com

Cover Art by *Rae Monet, Inc. Design*

The Wild Rose Press, Inc.
PO Box 708
Adams Basin, NY 14410-0708
Visit us at www.thewildrosepress.com

Publishing History
First Fantasy Rose Edition, 2020
Trade Paperback ISBN 978-1-5092-3393-9
Digital ISBN 978-1-5092-3394-6

Hotel LaBelle, Book 4
Published in the United States of America

Dedication

This book is dedicated to all the Missing and Murdered Indigenous Women (MMIW). Every Native American family has been touched by this epidemic and it is time for our nation to come together to stop it. No family should suffer this kind of pain.

~*~

It is also dedicated with love to my first reader and husband, Dale, and to our son, Joshua, our daughter-in-law, Elyse, our grandson, Dexter, and our granddaughter, Charlotte. They remind me every day that family ties bind with love and priceless memories—and that bond should never be ripped apart.

~*~

It is also dedicated to my tireless and supportive editor, Amanda Barnett, who is my book midwife, helping to bring my book babies into the world.

~*~

And to Sharon Saracino, my funny and fun critique partner and friend. She helps me see the humor in all things in the writing life and other parts of my sometimes crazy world.

Prologue

Crow Reservation, Billings, Montana

Jacob Graywolf walked in the door at six on Friday evening. Jessie, the gray-chinned black Labrador mix, greeted him with a slow wave of her tail and slumped down at his feet. "How you doing, old girl?" He rubbed her head, and she gave him a doggy grin. "Biscuit?"

Her head jerked up, and her tail thumped. "Here you go." He dug a treat out of the jar. "The way you like it."

Setting a bouquet of flowers on the table, he placed his black-padded jacket on the hook and looped his Sam Browne over the next one. The belt with his holstered side-arm hadn't bothered him all day. The moment he arrived home, however, it seemed as if the tools of his career—even the light-weight Kevlar vest—weighed a hundred pounds.

The tantalizing aroma of roasting turkey filled the kitchen, and his stomach growled in anticipation of a feast.

Rummaging under the sink to find a suitable vase, Jacob's hand fell on the one he'd made for his mother in middle school using the class pottery wheel. Streaks of blue and red drizzled down the sides, cooked into perpetual tears by the kiln. *Perfect.* After he trimmed the ends of the stems and removed the greenery that would slide beneath the surface and hasten the decaying process, a thorn pricked his index finger and a rivulet of crimson sluiced into the water. With his dry hand, he pulled out a tissue and pressed it to the weeping wound.

He placed the red roses in the center of the table set with three place settings, a braided loaf of challah, and two unlit white tapers. A whisper of a sound, and his mother entered the kitchen—wrapped in a colorful, geometric-patterned dress, her long, dark hair still damp.

"Jacob! You're early. And you brought my favorite flowers." She pecked him on the cheek, and the scent of eucalyptus washed over him reminding him of his asthma treatments as a child. "You must've gone all the way into Billings for them. Thank you."

"No, Mom. I'm on time. And you're welcome."

She smiled and waved a hand as if swatting a fly. "That's early in this house."

"Only for you." He glanced at his watch. "How long before dinner is ready? Do I have time to grab a quick shower?"

"Yes. I even left you some hot water."

As he headed toward his wing of the house, she called after him. "I can't wait to tell you about this new doctor at the clinic. What a jerk."

"Now, Mom, you were a tenderfoot once, too." He chuckled. Every July, the same complaint was issued when a fresh batch of doctors and nurses arrived at the Crow Indian Health Service to repay their student loans. His mother, a nurse midwife, had been on the reservation for over three decades, and she could spot the good, bad, and ugly ones the day they hit the door. Her predictions were eerily on target. "This one's a keeper. That one will only last three months and ask to be transferred. That one is dangerous. I'll have to watch him like a hawk."

Nine times out of ten, she was right. The one time she'd been wrong had been a doozy. She'd planned to stay at the clinic for three years—but never left.

Twenty minutes later, scrubbed clean of road dust, traffic stops, and disorderly conduct calls, Jacob began carving the turkey for their Sabbath dinner while his mother arranged all of the side dishes on the table.

"Is that huckleberry sauce, I hope?" His mouth watered. Sweeter than cranberries, and tarter than blueberries, the hard-to-gather fruit was one of his favorites.

"Why, yes, it is. I had to fight off three black bears to get enough." She put her hand on her chest before continuing, "But for you and your father, no effort is too hard."

"Miriam Oldhand had a good harvest?"

She laughed. "Yes. She did." She picked up her story from earlier. "I'm telling you. What a day at the clinic. Endless. And that new doctor?"

He sipped his water and nodded, knowing not to interrupt his mother in her narrator mode. "Something's not right about that boy. Even the mice avoid him."

"Mom!" Jacob laughed. "You're not supposed to say things like that."

She harrumphed. "I don't like his great-white-savior attitude, as if we haven't been able to get along without him for all these years."

"Cut him some slack, Mom. You were new once, too, and out of your element. Lay some of your wisdom on him, show him the way."

Her expression softened. "You're like your father, always giving people the benefit of the doubt."

A wave of sadness crested and crashed within him. It had been over twenty years since his death, and *still* she spoke of his father in the present tense. A testament to the enduring power of love? An inability to move on with her life? Or was it, as she said, that Joseph Graywolf had never truly left them.

"Dad was Chief of the Crow Tribe, a politician. People loved him. I'm a cop. People hate to see me coming."

"You're both leaders. And people love you. I know because they tell me so at the clinic, all the time."

He placed slices of the bird on the waiting serving platter, cut the sweet potatoes in half, and slathered them with cinnamon butter and brown sugar. *Sweet potato pies, minus the crust, the way his father liked them.* Maybe they were more alike than he recalled.

"Ready?"

She nodded, and then lit the traditional Jewish Sabbath candles and chanted the Hebrew blessing. *"Baruch atah Adonai Eloheinu, Melech haolam, asher kid'shanu b'mitzvotav, v'tzivanu l'hadlik ner shel Shabbat.* Blessed are you, Adonai our God, Sovereign of all, who hallows us with this mitzvot, commanding us to kindle the light of Sabbath."*

The door flew open, the candles blew out, and his mother's face paled. "Joseph," she breathed.

Chuffing softly, Jessie lumbered to her feet, her tail wagging in greeting.

Jacob strained his eyes, to no avail. Unable to see spirits, he had to rely on his mother—and the dog—to alert him to their presence. "What is he saying?"

She shook her head, her gaze never leaving the open doorway. "He's not speaking—his face—it's covered in blood." She turned to her son. "You need to get back to work. Someone's been murdered."

Chapter One

Crow Reservation, Billings, Montana

Jacob stared at the map spread out on the table in the conference room. A lump the size of a baseball lodged in his throat. No matter how often he saw them, the red pushpins piercing the nametags of the Missing and Murdered Indigenous Women or MMIWs in Montana and Wyoming moved him close to tears. Willing himself not to cry, he rubbed his eyes pretending lack of sleep, not an excess of emotion. The latest death wasn't an MMIW case, and it wasn't a murder, contrary to his mother's ominous warning—but rather from natural causes.

Tommy Otterlegs, a member of the Crow Nation and a Deputy Sheriff with Yellowstone County and the deceased's brother, asked with a tremor in his voice, "Who found Coral?"

Jacob placed his hand on the shorter man's shoulder. "Eddy."

"Poor kid," Tommy said with long exhale. "He already has a lot of issues at school. Father's in jail for life, now his mother is dead. Do we know what happened?"

"When I arrived at Coral's house, Eddy was sitting next to her on the ground, holding her hand and stroking her hair." Jacob paused. He'd lost his father at the same age. The worst day of his life—yet he couldn't recall a single thing about that night. Would Eddy have the same response to his parent's death? It might be a blessing if he could black out the moment he found her, until he was old enough to process his emotions—and reactions.

The kid was a wild child, Coral's one and only boy, big for his age, spoiled, and headstrong. In Jacob's experience, after a trauma of this nature, some kids became depressed and withdrawn, others became angry and acted out. He guessed they'd find out soon enough which way Eddy would go. "He was quiet, calm. In shock, I think. Apparently, Coral had been hanging out the laundry and collapsed."

"They're going to miss her at the elementary school. She was a popular teacher—everybody loved Coral." Tommy choked up. "I can't believe my sister is dead. We were close, you know? My mother is devastated."

"I'm so sorry for your loss. I'll miss her, too. She was one of my favorite cousins." His heart twisted in his chest, aching for Tommy, watching him struggle to remain calm. Telling people their loved one was gone from their lives chipped away at his heart every time. Today was especially poignant—and personal. He had to keep it together, not lose control of his emotions. Later, tonight perhaps, but not now.

"What did the medical examiner say?" Tommy clenched his Deputy Sheriff hat in his hands so hard, his knuckles turned white.

"Natural causes." At his cousin's questioning expression, Jacob elaborated. "A heart attack. You know Joe Hager, good ME, all brains, but zero people sense. Gave me a lecture, told me it's the most common cause of death for Native Americans and a third of our people die under the age of sixty-five from heart disease."

"She was only forty-two," Tommy protested. "She had a whole life ahead of her."

"I know." Jacob cocked his head to one side, puzzled. "There was one odd finding—fresh stitches at the base of her neck, right at the hairline."

Tommy frowned. "Stitches?"

Jacob nodded. "New. Like this past week. Did she mention any plans for a surgical procedure to you?"

"I haven't spoken with Coral since our baby naming. Between work and home and trying to help Wanda—" Tommy choked up "—I've been tied up, you know?"

"I do know." He wondered how often he'd speak with his mother if he didn't live at home with her. "When will you have the funeral? I'd like to come."

"I have to talk to my mother. I'm guessing sooner rather than later. And I need to take care of Eddy." Tommy shook his head. "To be honest, the kid is a hand full. With the new baby and Wanda being up half the night, I don't know how having a fourth grader who's always in trouble in our house is going to work out."

"What about your mother? Can she take him in?"

"She's over seventy and her arthritis is killing her. Doesn't keep her from cooking, cleaning, and bead work." He shrugged. "I'll discuss it with her, see what she thinks. Eddy won't be without a home, but I'm not sure which of us will take him."

"Maybe you and your mother can take turns riding

herd on him." Roping and wrangling Eddy Little Bear was closer to the truth, but Jacob kept that nugget of advice to himself.

"Yeah." He nodded. "Thanks. Say hi to your mom for me."

As Tommy ambled out the door with slumped shoulders, his normal jaunty bantam rooster strut gone, Jacob's cell phone rang.

"Jacob, this is Hal Wiley. Is Tommy still with you?"

"He's about to walk out the door."

Tommy paused mid-step and turned.

"Tell him his nephew is here with me in Billings. He's just been arrested for shoplifting."

"I'm putting you on speaker, Hal." He held the phone up. "What did Eddy steal?"

"Walked out of the grocery store with three steaks stuffed into his pants. Said he was hungry."

Tommy stared at the phone. "What's the bail?"

"A hundred bucks and he's yours until his court date," Hal responded. "As soon as I found out it was Eddy, I called the store, told the manager he was only nine years old, and he'd lost his mother this week. But the guy insisted on pressing charges. I'm sorry, Tommy. I know you don't need this right now."

Tommy sighed. "I'm on my way."

Hal said, "Don't hang up, Jacob. I have a proposition for you. I'd like you to serve on a taskforce to address our MMIW epidemic, be more proactive, less reactive."

"Isn't it being run out of Helena?"

"The bigger one is. And as you know it's a three-hour drive to Helena. Our mayor felt we should have a local group reporting to the one in the capitol, thinks we'll have a better grassroots response."

"Who's on it?" Of course, he'd say yes, it was one of his top priorities, but he wanted to know which agencies he'd be working with.

"Tommy's supposed to be on it, but he'll be out for a while. Chairman Dan will be there, along with representatives from other tribes. Then there's the police chief, and the city administrator. I think he's there to make sure we don't vote to encumber funds from the city." He paused. "And there's an FBI representative, too."

"I don't know whether to offer my congratulations or my condolences." Notorious for taking over cases and not sharing information with the local law enforcement officers, the FBI was not always welcome at the table. "Why would they send someone to us? Shouldn't they be working with the Helena taskforce? And only if there's been an actual crime?"

"Don't sound so excited," Hal said dryly. "Our buddy, Bert Blackfeather, suggested we invite this one to join us as a consultant."

"Bert?" He liked and trusted the man, even attended his wedding. Jacob also knew he ran a shadowy division in Homeland Security—one that specialized in agents with supernatural talents. "Why would he be involved in this?"

"Don't look a gift horse in the mouth. I know you now have access to the National Crime Information Center with the Tribal Assistance Program grant. But the feds have resources we can only *dream* of having."

"Maybe they're sending some guy in a suit for show?"

Hal blew out a long breath. "Gal in a suit."

"Great. Can't wait to meet her." Jacob grimaced. The last female FBI agent he had worked with had been six-foot-two inches tall, built like a grizzly bear, and about as friendly.

"So, you'll do it?"

"Sure. I haven't been tortured by the FBI in a while. What's the worst she can do to me?"

****

Billings Logan International Airport
Billings, Montana

Zena Adalwolf checked her watch a second time and scanned the conveyor belt for her black bag. *Like the sign says, many bags look alike—except mine.* She lunged at the large suitcase with the leopard duct tape wrapped around the handle. Not FBI standard issue, but a standout on the conveyer belt. She slung her messenger bag with her computer across her torso and rolled her way to the rental car desk. After producing multiple forms of identification, including her badge to ensure she obtained the government rate, the goggling young clerk handed her the trifold paperwork, thanked her, and pointed her toward the parking lot.

As she neared the exit, the clerk said to the kid at the next counter in a low voice, "She's an FBI agent? Don't they have height requirements? She's no bigger than my kid sister. I wouldn't mind dating her, though. I love redheads."

She kept walking, pretending she hadn't heard him from across the crowded space. Back in the day, she would have turned and called him out with, "I don't date little boys" but she'd discovered on a stakeout of some mobsters that her uncanny hearing ability gave her an edge over bad guys. Her colleagues attributed her inside knowledge to lip reading. It was more believable than telling them she could hear someone from a block away—and smell emotions when she walked into a room. Of course, there were some disadvantages to these superpowers, like the odors of lust when some men saw her and hearing the same things with a million variations on the same theme— *outcast.*

"Oh, you're an FBI agent? How cute."

"Since when did the feds start hiring leprechauns?"

"Where's your partner? Who's going to protect you?"

"Where's the real agent on this case?"

Over time, she'd learned to let the comments roll off her back. Biting people's heads off didn't score points with colleagues or bosses, so she smiled, swallowed her remarks, and proved them wrong. *Every. Single. Time.*

Once upon a time, she'd been in law school focused on social justice preparing to help the vulnerable and underserved. Then one small decision to stay home to study instead of going out for a hike changed her life. After that fateful summer, Zena had decided the best way to use her education and experience was with the FBI. Armed with a grim resolve and obsessive dedication to investigate and solve women's abductions and deaths, she would not be bound by other people's preconceived notions. Her family, however, was another matter. At graduation, when she announced she had joined the FBI, her extended family had been appalled. She was supposed to come home and help run the family businesses. Not one Adalwolf had *ever* been in law enforcement. The clan had looked down their long noses at her and sniffed with disdain. Now, only her father, mother, and kid brothers spoke with her and even those conversations were stilted and painful.

Her mother said with each call, "Hi, honey. I spoke with Aaron." Aaron was a guy Zena had dated in high school. "He asks about you all the time. When will you be coming home again?"

Zena's answer was always the same. "Mom, I know you mean well, but it would never work out. Not one of the guys in Summertown is remotely interested in me."

She was not like them and never would be. *Outcast.*

Tossing her bag into the back of the black SUV, she drove out of the airport parking lot, down the hill, and into the city. Seven minutes later, the GPS announced her arrival at the Yellowstone County Sheriff's Office. *Quick and easy.*

After getting additional details from the local deputies, as well as the address for the meeting in the morning, she set the navigator to find Hotel LaBelle. It was late, she was tired, and she couldn't wait to grab a cold drink, climb into a hot shower, and fall into a soft bed. The photos from the website had been stunning. The Victorian structure did not disappoint, with the wrap around porch and rocking chairs inviting guests to spend lazy afternoons sipping tea. Mule deer grazed on the banks of the Yellowstone River, and the big Montana sky was filled with red, purple, and blue clouds.

The owners stood on the top step with welcoming smiles. Lucius Stewart, the handsome mustachioed man held his blonde wife, Tallulah, protectively wrapping his arm above the gentle swell of her belly. Beside her, a little red headed girl with mischief in her eyes stared straight at the camera with a lop-sided grin on her face. Some of the child's teeth were missing, making her all the more adorable. Being a ginger herself, Zena couldn't help but feel a kinship with the little tyke. After the events in Summertown, Bert Blackfeather had taken an interest in her studies and mentored her. He had assured her she would be welcome at the hotel. Unlike her clan, they looked like the all-American family. *Normal.*

Pulling off the highway onto the long, curving driveway, she paused a moment at the top of the hill to enjoy the view. It was better than she had imagined. She wondered what it would be like to come home to a sight like this every day. Would she get used to it, or would it take her breath away each time she crested the hill? She sighed and put the car in gear. Would she always be destined to be a nomad, travelling from place to place, shunned by her clan, never welcomed at home? Or was she ready to put roots down here and never look in her rear-view mirror again? Time to find out.

After she parked and removed her bags from the car, she headed toward the stairs. The front door opened and a beige and black sphere of fur hurtled toward her, piercing her ears with a banshee shriek.

"Don't mind Franny," Lucius called. "She's excitable but harmless."

"No alarm system required." She bent down and

offered the pug the back of her hand. Franny sniffed, took two steps back, tilted her head, and gave Zena a puzzled look. "Don't' worry," she crooned. "I promise not to bite."

The little dog ran up the stairs, sat behind her owner's feet, and peered around his leg.

"Well, I'll be," Lucius said. "First time I've ever seen Franny act that way. Usually, we can't get her off our guests, and I have to give out lint rollers because she sheds so much." The tall man loped down the stairs, grabbed Zena's large rolling bag, and led her to the entrance.

"Must have been something I said to make her run off," she said with a little laugh. "I'm Zena Adalwolf. Your place was highly recommended by Bert Blackfeather. If the inside is anything like the outside, you may never get rid of me."

"The Hotel LaBelle has that effect on people. Ask my darlin' wife, Tallulah."

The visibly pregnant blonde standing in the lobby greeted her guest with a smile. "I came here three years ago as a consultant—and never left."

"Consultant on what?" Zena asked.

"This place." Tallulah held her palms up and turned around. "It was a wreck. We have before and after photos we like to show off. Most people can't imagine how bad it was. Goats used to roam these halls."

The little redhead from the photos skipped into the lobby, stopped, and stared at Zena. "Who's the wolf lady, Mama?"

"Ms. Adalwolf is a guest, Miriam." Tallulah glanced at Zena. "We're not very formal here, but we do have *some* manners."

"No," the child said shaking her head. "She's a wolf, like Uncle Jacob. But different."

A man said, "Did I hear a little redheaded girl talking about me?"

The child shrieked like the pug had, and then flung herself into a uniformed man's open arms. "What did you bring me?"

"Why would you think I'd have something for you?"

She searched his shirt pocket, pulled out a packet of gum, and took off.

"Sugarless," he said to Tallulah with a wink. He turned his gaze on Zena.

Transfixed by the flash of quicksilver in his eyes, Zena inhaled a rush of scents—the woods in the fall, frost creeping over grass, a crisp snap in the air—and secrets. The heady mix threw her off guard—and then it hit her. Pure, unadulterated lust. But it wasn't his. It was *hers*. She wanted to search every inch of his body to find those differences, line up their similarities, and dive into the primal urge to take this man as her mate. She exhaled a long, slow breath she hadn't realized she'd been holding and watched as he extended his hand. His almost exquisite looking fingers were not what she expected from someone she assumed was a law enforcement officer. Their palms connected and Zena wanted to howl with delight and happiness—and fear as well.

This man who brought out the creature in Zena was a wolf shifter, too.

Chapter Two

Hotel LaBelle ~*~ Billings, Montana

As Jacob's palm connected with the petite woman's hand, goosebumps erupted up his arm, down to his toes, and all points in between. He forced himself to concentrate on her full red lips beneath the button nose covered with freckles. *What was she saying?* Her name. *Zena.* A warrior's name, a woman of valor's name, a name imbued with the power of her werewolf clan. He was certain she had given him her last name and title—details he should have been paying more attention to. But all he could see was her long, lovely throat, and the rosy skin leading down to her twin globes, barely contained by a white button-down shirt. Lust washed over him, hers mixed with his, and the urge to sweep her into his arms and take her upstairs to a big four-poster bed clawed at his groin. Visions of ripping her clothes off, kissing those lush lips, nuzzling her neck, biting and nipping at her shoulders, and molding her backside to his belly in frantic passionate mating clouded his mind.

Did she feel it, too? She had to. How could she not? Look at those big green eyes, pupils expanded. Her breath came faster, as did his. His longing screamed at him, nearly drowning out the voices of the others not in their bubble of desire.

Lucius' hearty voice cut through the fog of hormones, and Jacob tore his gaze away from Zena's.

"I had a feeling you two might hit it off right away, what with you both being in law enforcement."

Tallulah punched her husband in the arm. "Stop."

"What?" He gave her an innocent look. "Did I say something wrong?"

The connection broke. Jacob took a step back. Zena shook her head. *Now what?*

"Sorry, must be the jetlag." She gave a self-conscious laugh. "I lost track of the conversation. Let me try again. I'm Special Agent Zena Adalwolf. Our mutual friend, Bert Blackfeather, connected me with Hal Wiley, who asked me to meet with your local taskforce on MMIW. I've been given permission to assist you for a month—or a little more. I will help as much as I can during that timeframe."

Four weeks? He had only twenty-eight days to seduce, bed, and mate her? His mother would kill him if he treated any woman with such a callous calculation.

Tamping down his wilder side, he nodded and said, "We'll be happy with whatever time and assistance you can provide us."

"Jacob," Tallulah interjected. "Why don't we let Ms. Adalwolf get into her room and freshen up. It's a long trip from the east coast. I'm sure she must be starving."

Zena's face lit up. "I've been thinking about a hot shower since I stepped off the plane. How long until dinner?"

"Let's say thirty minutes or so? Gives me time to get Miriam to bed so we can have an adult conversation. Work for you?"

"I'll take your bags up to your room." Lucius placed a large hand on Jacob's shoulder. "Why don't you step into the saloon and grab a drink? I'll meet you there in a few minutes."

Jacob nodded and wandered off to his favorite room in the hotel. *What the hell was wrong with him?* He'd never had this intensity of attraction to a woman before. Sure, he'd had a few relationships, but no one had gripped his body and brains this fiercely the first time he'd met them. After grabbing a soft drink for himself and a glass of pinot noir for Lucius, he took them to a table, and admired the room. With the long marble bar, the brass rail, a player piano in the corner, and the antique jackalope, deer, bison, and bear heads on the wall, the room came right out of another era. He pulled out his cell phone and did a quick Internet search.

Game over.

Lucius loped over to the table, plopped into a chair, and sipped at his wine. "She is one fine looking filly, don't you agree?"

"Too rich for my blood."

Lucius slammed his hand on the table. "What in tarnation are you talking about? She's perfect for you. I've never seen you look at a woman that way."

Jacob handed his phone to his friend. "Read it and weep."

"Adalwolf Winery, established in the eighteen-hundreds, has been in the Adalwolf family for over two-hundred years. In addition to the vineyards, the family offers extensive event venues for discerning clientele seeking destination weddings. Summertown, West Virginia is surrounded by rolling hills, acres of state forests and rivers suitable for hiking, biking, camping, and whitewater rafting. Interested parties should contact *AdalwolfInfo@AdalwolfEnterprises.com*"

Lucius looked up from the screen, a grin playing on his face. "She's one of a kind, cowboy. Why would you let a little thing like her having money get in your way?"

Heat flushed Jacob's cheeks. "I've been burned before. Little rich girl playing on the wrong side of the tracks—takes off when things get serious. You think her family is going to allow her to be with a poor Indian guy like me?"

"You know what happens when you assume?" Lucius asked. "You make an ass—"

Jacob's temper flared. "This is an educated guess, not an assumption. She's leaving town in a month. What kind of chance could I possibly have with her?"

"I hate to say it," Tallulah said from the doorway, "but Lucius is right. You have more in common than you're letting on. Miriam spotted it right away. And if I'm not mistaken, you guys recognized you are mates on contact."

"Dang!" Lucius slapped his thigh. "Mark the calendar. My wife said I was right. I knew you two were meant for each other. Those sparks lit up the lobby."

Jacob drank the rest of his soda in one gulp. "I'm not sure which one of you is crazier."

Lucius tapped the side of his head. "Like a fox."

Jacob stood. "I'd best be on my way."

"Aren't you staying for dinner?" Tallulah protested. "It's only us. Season is over, there are no other guests. I set the kitchen table for four people."

"I don't think it's a good idea." Truth be told, the urge to mate with Zena had been so overwhelming, he didn't trust himself to be too close to her in an informal setting. "I have to work with her. I can't run the risk of even the appearance of impropriety."

Tallulah sighed. "Your mother raised you right, Jacob Graywolf. Give Esther a hug for me when you get home."

Metal clanged on metal and Lucius glanced toward the lobby. "You'd best skedaddle, then. She's coming down the elevator as we speak."

Jacob almost ran in his haste to get out of the bar and into the lobby. He tipped his hat at the pixie inside the brass and wood cage of the elevator, closed the heavy front door, and breathed a sigh of relief. He'd avoided making a fool of himself. Never again would he allow his animal side to cloud his judgement. He was a lone wolf. Only a few close friends, others with secrets like his, knew. He'd given his heart once before, an out of state visitor who had heard Indians made the best lovers. When he tried to take the relationship to the next level, she'd laughed at him. *Summer fun*. That's what she'd called it. Nothing more. He'd been mortified. He'd worked hard to get past that humiliation—and to become Chief of Tribal Police. No one, not even a woman as rare as this one, would make him commit emotional or professional suicide.

****

Zena stepped out of the vintage brass and wood elevator and cast a longing look at Jacob's back through the glass pane of the front door. "He's in a hurry. Did he get a call?"

21

"He's always in a rush, can't even stay for dinner." Tallulah smiled and led her to the large eat-in kitchen. "Is your room okay?'

"Better than okay. It's wonderful. I love the claw foot tub and that big four-poster. I can't wait to fall into it tonight." She placed her phone on the big wooden table and slid into a chair while her hostess pulled an iron skillet out of the oven. The heavenly aroma of poultry spices filled the air. "I have a question—I hate to even ask this."

"I know, you want some of my espresso." Lucius patted the gleaming machine. "This baby can make whatever you want. Decaf? Regular? Cappuccino? Latte? I'm your huckleberry."

"That is one impressive coffee maker. After dinner, maybe a decaf latte?" She picked up her smartphone, tapped the screen, and held it out to Tallulah and Lucius. "Does your daughter have access to your guest rooms?"

Tallulah stared at the photo and sighed. "No, and before you ask, that's not her."

"She doesn't have a mask that looks like an—"

"Ugly little man?" Lucius leaped in. "Honey, this is your territory."

"Hold on," Tallulah griped. "Let me get the food on the table, then we can talk." The hot pan of fried chicken landed on a tile trivet, followed by a steaming basket of biscuits and a large bowl of spinach salad. "Butter, salt, and pepper are on the table, along with water. What am I missing?"

"This," Lucius said, and plunked a small jar next to his plate. "I can't eat biscuits without my favorite jam."

"Wow. You eat like this every night?" Zena

marveled. "I'd be as big as a house."

"Out here in Big Sky Country, you work it off." Tallulah patted her belly. "Plus, I'm eating for two."

Distracted by the juicy flavor of fresh fried chicken, Zena tucked into the meal as if she hadn't eaten in weeks. When was the last time she'd had chicken and biscuits? The heck with the healthy green stuff, *this* was heaven. She closed her eyes, and her taste buds sang, begging for more.

"Tallulah's cooking is a bit of a religious experience, isn't it?" Lucius chuckled. "This is a warm-up. Wait 'til you have breakfast."

Startled out of her food induced fugue, Zena nodded, wiped her chin, and laughed. "You caught me. So, about that picture on my phone. If it's not your daughter, who is it?"

Tallulah twisted in her chair. "Come on, she won't bite you. What? I don't know if she can see you. You owe her an apology."

Who is she talking to? Is she hallucinating? Lucius doesn't look the least bit concerned.

"How many times have we had this conversation?" The blonde frowned and shook her head. "I'm serious. This is not a joke."

"Who is she talking to?" Zena said to Lucius in a low voice.

"Bohpoli," he responded and slathered more butter and jam on a biscuit. "He's a prankster. Loves to take selfies."

Because, sure, an invisible man taking his picture is normal.

"Say you're sorry like you mean it," Tallulah continued. "Do you like getting us in trouble? The last guest did *not* think it was funny. He was so angry, we had to give him a refund."

"He'll never learn, Tallulah." Lucius grabbed a crispy golden leg. "He can't help himself. Be grateful he limits it to playing with electronic gadgets. Could be worse."

"Finally," Tallulah huffed. "He said he's sorry. Like pulling teeth."

"Ahem." Zena cleared her throat loudly. "Could someone *please* tell me what's going on?"

"I'm sure you've noticed by now that we aren't a normal family," Tallulah said.

"Had me fooled—well except for when Miriam met me." Zena bit her bottom lip. "That was a little…odd."

"Let's back up this horse and buggy." Lucius wiped his moustache with his napkin. "How do you know Bert Blackfeather? He's Homeland Security, you're FBI. What's the connection?"

"Friend of the family," Zena said. *Did she say that too quickly?*

"That so?" Lucius gave her a skeptical look. "I don't recollect him ever mentioning the Adalwolfs."

Tallulah patted her husband's hand. "Don't be rude. We can't possibly know all of Bert's friends, even if we are related."

Related? Now this was an interesting turn of events.

As if reading her mind, Tallulah added, "By marriage. Lucius is Bert's—what is it honey? Great-great-great-great. Whatever. Grandfather. And Bert is Emma Horserider's brother—she's a horse trainer. She's married to Bronco Winchester. They have eighteen-month old twins, Emily and Adam." She rolled her eyes. "Talk about pranksters. Then there's Beautiful Blackfeather. She's a medicine woman. I'm sure you'll get to meet her at some point. She likes to pop in every now and again."

"Can you go back a bit?" Zena looked between her two hosts, wondering if this was a *folie a deux*, where both people shared a common delusion. "You meant Bert and Lucius are related *through* an ancestor, right? Not that he's Bert's paternal grandfather?"

Lucius reached for another biscuit. "Maternal. Beautiful was my mother-in-law."

"The one you said might drop in?"

Tallulah nodded. "Exactly. We have a complicated family most people wouldn't understand." She favored Zena with a meaningful look. "But *you're* not most people."

"Lucius," she asked. "How old are you?"

He grinned. "How old do you think I am?"

"Forty-ish?" She held her breath and waited for his response.

"Add a century to that number and you'd hit the nail on the head." He held his hand up. "Now, let me explain."

Lucius recounted how he'd been the original owner of Hotel LaBelle, but his first wife, Mourning Dove, had died in childbirth. Beautiful Blackfeather, his mother-in-law, had come to the hotel and cursed him. He could only be released from limbo when he found a woman he loved more than his hotel. He patted Tallulah's hand. "This here fine woman freed me from an eternity of roaming these halls all alone."

"Is Beautiful still alive?"

Tallulah laughed so hard she snorted. "Some days it feels like it, but no. She's a spirit, an extremely powerful ghost, who likes to be with her family."

The ugly little man. What about him? "Bohpoli? Is he a dead relative, too?"

"Oh, no." Tallulah waved her hand as if swatting a fly. "He's like family, though. He's training Miriam to become a medicine woman. He doesn't permit everyone to see him. He's a Choctaw supernatural—that's his job."

"Your daughter is a—"

"Thunderbird," Lucius cut in. "Awfully powerful. That's why she needs to be taught right."

"We have huckleberry cobbler for dessert." Tallulah pulled a glass dish out of the oven. "Who wants vanilla ice cream with that?"

Medicine women. Supernatural pranksters. Ghosts. Thunderbirds. A century-old hotel owner. Huckleberry cobbler for dessert. A normal family dinner conversation. Or was it?

"Do you two work for Bert in the Anomaly Defense Division?"

"Well, I'll be doggone." Lucius clapped his hands. "So, you know all about that?"

"Not everything. What are your talents?" *Dive into the crazy and swim with the current.* "And, yes, I'd love some ice cream."

Tallulah placed a generous scoop on the plump pastry and purple filling and set it in front of Zena. "I see ghosts—and supernaturals—like Bohpoli. And I do a little remote viewing. Not as much as Bronco. He's better at it than I am."

"Honey, you're much more talented than you let

on." Lucius snagged a plate and plopped into his chair. "Besides, he has Gaucho. I'm the least talented of our bunch. I have to use Beautiful's medicine stick to become invisible. I'm no good without the dag-blasted thing."

Tallulah sat down with a small portion of the dessert and kissed her husband. "I wouldn't say you're useless. You've given me a home and two babies."

Jealousy spiked in Zena's chest. *If only.*

"So, tell us." Lucius raised his craggy eyebrows. "Is everyone in your family a werewolf?"

Chapter Three

Crow Indian Health Service ~*~ *Crow Agency, Montana*

Esther Graywolf glanced up as the new doctor, Brett Turner, strutted through the clinic's morning hive of activity. He flipped his shock of blond hair off his forehead, raised his chin, and puffed his chest out. Not one word of greeting to any of the patients. *What an arrogant ass.*

She returned to her conversation with Mary, her LPN co-worker.

"So sad," Esther commented. "Only in her forties. Poor Eddy found her."

"Who are you guys talking about?" Turner interjected. "Is it one of our patients?"

Esther ground her teeth. *As if he cared.* He was being nosey.

Puffy faced, red-eyed, Mary sniffed. "Coral Little Bear died of a heart attack."

He put his hand on his chest. "No, that's *terrible*. I saw her few days ago for migraines." He paused and shook his head. "Oh dear, I'm so sorry. I know I shouldn't discuss her health care. I'm—I'm stunned."

"It's a shock to all of us," Esther said, and patted the other woman's shoulder. "Back to work. I have a lot of pregnant ladies to see today." She turned and bumped into him. "You need something, Doctor?"

"Why yes, I do. Drug samples. Do we get any of those here, you know, to give out to patients who can't afford them?"

"You've been here three months, right?" She wanted to chalk his ignorance up to be being new, like Jacob had recommended. But something about the man irritated her so much, she found it challenging to interact with him. "We're not permitted to accept or distribute drug samples to our patients. Everything is in our pharmacy as part of their health care. Wasn't that information included in your orientation? If not, we need to let the administrator know so we can correct it."

"Silly me." He tapped his forehead. "You're right." He paused. "Ms. Graywolf, I have a professional question."

"Yes?"

"Whatever happened to nurses being in awe of physicians? You know, treating us nicely and bringing us coffee, that sort of thing?"

"Well, Doctor Turner," she said without changing her tone of voice, "nurses like me have the same number of years of education as you do, so we're equals now. Maybe *you* should be getting *me* a cup of coffee?"

"Yeah, right." He snorted, turned on his heel, and walked away, shaking his head.

"That guy—" Esther grumbled to Mary, "—is a bona fide jerk. Mark my words, he won't last a year."

The middle-aged woman gazed after him with a wistful expression. "Oh, I don't know. I think he's kinda cute. He's new, Esther, still learning the job. Like me."

"You earned that license, Mary. Not everyone has the courage to go back to school later in life like you did. You're doing a great job. Don't put yourself down." She tapped the counter. "It's not his looks that are my concern. I can't put my finger on why. He never says the *wrong* thing—but he's challenging, provocative, and not in a good way."

"I like him better than the other new guy. He's always grouchy."

"Beggars can't be choosers." Esther shrugged. "All we can do is pray they don't kill anyone while they're here. It's like winning the lottery when we get a good one."

"Got that right." Mary checked the schedule. "Francis Deerfoot is running late. A client didn't show up to court, so she had to run him down. Then her kid was sent home from school with a fever. Should we skip to the next patient?"

"Sure, we can take care of Francis when she gets here."

The day passed quickly as it always did when they were overbooked. Truth be told, Esther preferred busy to slow times, and she hated the boredom of downtime. She knew she should be used to it, after all. The life of a midwife consisted of hours of waiting for a child to be born and minutes of terror getting the baby out. Despite advances in medicine, pregnancy and childbirth were still the most dangerous time in woman's life—especially women of color.

As the last patient for the day walked out, and a cleaning lady walked in to mop the floor, Esther caught sight of Doctor Robert Mann, his cell phone glued to his ear. A teddy bear of a guy who worked well with anxiety ridden kids, while the adolescents loved him. When he first arrived, parents hadn't been so sure they'd wanted an openly gay man treating their children.

Accepting a Two Spirit who was born into the tribe was one thing, a mother had told Esther, but having one take care of their child alone in an exam room? That was another matter altogether. Esther sighed. Their loss. The guy was smart, a Rhodes scholar, or so the clinic administrator had said. At least the majority of parents had grown to trust him. Thank God. The remainder, a vocal minority, had elected to have their kids see the other doctor. The smarmy, too handsome for his own good one. He may have fooled some people, but he didn't fool her.

Robert's voice grew louder, now almost a shout. "What do you mean there's no way to fix this? I don't know how you could have screwed up this badly. I want to speak with your supervisor. She's gone for the day. When will she return? What's her direct number?"

Esther slipped past him, waved goodbye, and walked out to her car. His husband, she'd heard, was supposed to be placed with Robert here in Billings. Instead, he was in Arizona, thousands of miles away. A bureaucratic snafu *par excellence*. She hoped they could be together soon. Robert's misery radiated off of him when she walked by, much like that other doctor's arrogance and disdain—a sticky tentacle, wrapping itself around her throat. She shuddered. If only she could heal mental disorders the way she healed physical problems.

Today had been a good day. Frances Deerfoot, a defense lawyer and Vice Chairman of the Tribe, had shown up late with her sick child. In addition to his fever, he had a runny nose and nasty cough. Esther had turfed the kid to peds for an urgent visit. The enormously pregnant mother had complained of discomfort. Everyone was uncomfortable at eight months, but this had been different. Upon exam, it was clear the baby's head was not where it needed to be. With time, effort, and some focused healing vibes, when the mom left with antibiotics for her six-year old, the infant's head was down, and she was much more comfortable. *A good day.*

Esther pulled into her driveway to the unmistakable screeches of a great horned owl. *Tiger.* She'd know his call anywhere. He was in trouble. *Please don't be a bobcat.* Esther ran into her house, grabbed her Mossberg, and raced to the back of her lot where the bird nested. Tiger swooped and clawed—not at a four-legged animal, but a two legged one.

"Eddy Little Bear," she shouted, "get down from that tree *right now.*"

****

Jacob drove up to his house thirty minutes after his mother's call. That woman. Zena. She flitted in and out of his mind like a butterfly. *Mysterious. Beautiful. Alluring. Elusive.* He could not stop thinking about her. The trouble call, from his own home, had been a welcome respite from staring at his computer screen while reading the resumés of all the people on the task force. Repeatedly, he'd circled back to Zena Adalwolf's remarkable career—and life. Yet what he found off the Internet was more intriguing than what was on the screen. He'd needed Bert's help for that deep background information. It explained a lot, especially her intensity and drive to protect women. He sighed. Back to business.

Bandaged from elbow to wrist on his left arm, the little miscreant sat at his kitchen table, in his chair, eating his mother's pot roast, and mopping it up with her challah. Eddy did not look the least bit concerned that he was sitting in the home of the Tribal Chief of Police, facing the possibility of yet another court date. In fact, the only thing Eddy said was, "Could I have some more, please?"

"Mom." Jacob sighed. "You said you had a trespasser. Now you're giving him stew?"

"He was trying to get to Tiger's nest. He was looking for eggs. He's hungry." She refilled the kid's bowl. "I'm feeding him. Is that illegal?"

Tossing his shaggy black hair out of his eyes, Eddy grinned, his teeth a bright white contrast with the line of brown stew on his upper lip. "Your mom sure knows how to cook."

He cocked his head toward the bedroom. "Can we have a word?"

As soon as he closed the door, she said, "Tiger got his arm with his talons."

"The bird was defending his mate and nest."

"I know. I told Eddy he was lucky he didn't get his face torn off. He said, 'I'd look like Chairman Redhawk if I did.' " She shook her head. "Anyway, I cleaned the cuts and put some extra healing power on the wound. He'll have a small scar, but it will be better soon."

Jacob shook his head. "That kid's always in trouble."

"He's your cousin. You know that, right? Your father's family?"

"Yes, a teasing cousin. I know, but you called me here, and it's clear you have it all handled. What do you want me to do?"

"Can you get those shoplifting charges dropped?"

"The City of Billings is not my jurisdiction. Hal Wiley tried to reason with the manager of the grocery store. No deal."

"He only stole the steaks because he was hungry." She grabbed his hand. "Did you see how short his pants are? He's growing like a weed in the summer—and who's cooking for him? Wanda! I've had her food. It's *not* good. She thinks one grocery store rotisserie chicken serves ten people."

"Not everyone cooks like you—or as much as you do."

"Your father's family always served more food than anyone could finish. And Jews do not allow people to leave their home hungry." Tears welled in her eyes. "That child is starving."

"Tommy's got a lot on his plate right now. Coral's death. Wanda. A baby. Eddy." He blew out a long breath. "It's a lot to ask of anyone."

"Eddy told me Wanda doesn't like him."

"I'm sure he's exaggerating."

Jacob's mother had always been a soft touch when it came to the injured and weak. He'd never forget when she brought Tiger home. An owlet, barely able to hop around, his wing broken. She'd defied her husband who kept repeating, "He brings messages of death" and instead kept the owl. Setting up a little house for him with a warming lightbulb, she tended to the bird's wounds, fed him, and concentrated her healing touch on his injury. Jacob had helped, bringing live mice for the raptor to eat each day. At last, the bird had been able to fly on his own. But he never went far, always returning to his little house—until he took a mate. As if tethered to the property, he'd set up his nest close enough to the house to stop by and visit and far enough away to have some privacy. His territory encompassed their home. Esther and Jacob welcomed this noisy tiger-of-the-sky member of the family.

"What about his grandmother? Do you think she could take him in? It's been a month since Coral died. She must be lonely. Eddy would be good company for her," his mother spoke up again.

"I think you're projecting. His grandmother is one of the busiest women on the rez. She's the lead in every beading, blanket, or elk-tooth dress project." He shook his head. "I'm not sure she'd welcome *this* little bundle of joy."

"He said the other kids pick on him at school. Called him *Special Eddy* because he can't read at grade level." She dabbed her eyes. "Dyslexia. Children can be so cruel. I'd hate to see this sweet little boy getting into—you know—there are a lot of bad influences out there."

She didn't have to say the word. *Drugs.* An epidemic of opioids and meth raced ahead of law enforcement. It was like playing whack-a-mole. They'd put one dealer away—and another would pop up. The other day, they'd arrested a pair of young women traveling from another reservation with heroin. *Heroin.* As if things weren't bad enough with meth.

He pulled her in for a hug. "How about we keep him for the night? I'll call Tommy, let him know Eddy's here so he won't be worried. Things will look better in the morning. I'll talk to his grandmother. See what she thinks. Okay?"

She nodded. "Thanks, Jacob. You're the best son in the world."

"That's cheating." He laughed. "I'm your only son. You have to say that."

"But I mean it. I'm blessed and I know it."

"Let's go back to the kitchen, see if our guest has eaten us out of house and home, shall we?"

His mother led the way, stopped, and smiled.

Snoring lightly, Eddy slept with his head on the table, and a smile on his face.

Chapter Four

City Hall ~~ Billings, Montana*

Twenty minutes ahead of the scheduled meeting time, Zena surveyed the empty conference room and claimed her favorite spot. Her back to the wall, cattycornered from the door and the head of the table, she had a wide-angle view of the meeting space. The vantage point gave her the opportunity to note who arrived when and what chair they chose. Table politics played an important role in every committee, task force, and organization. She'd know who outranked whom by the seating arrangement. Placing her tablet next to her extra-large latte and mentally thanking Lucius for the to-go cup, she reviewed her notes on the participants—keen to see the faces that matched the names.

A middle-aged man with graying temples, eyeglasses, and a ready smile was first to enter and introduce himself as Reid Wood, the city administrator. He took the seat at the head of the table by the window. *Large and in charge.* Zena glanced at his resume. Master's in Public Administration, Certificate in City Administration. A wife, three kids, enjoys hiking—of course, it's Montana—and collecting antiques. He wore an aftershave with a woodsy scent and thankfully, not too much of the scent. No odor of lust coming off him. *Good.* He was happy at home and wouldn't bother her.

Dressed in a black uniform, a tall, lean man with gray hair and a moustache, entered the room, said hello to Reid, and introduced himself to Zena as Hal Wiley, the Yellowstone County Sheriff. His rugged good looks were a touch older than his online photo, but he still had charisma and an appealing smile. He had probably rocked a few women out of their cowboy boots in his day. No aftershave, thank God, and not a hint of lechery. *Yay. Two for two.*

A middle-aged man with a horseshoe of salt and pepper hair surrounding his bald pate entered the room along with a hint of a cherry scent. *Pipe tobacco in his pocket?* He too wore a black uniform. His name tag said Chief James. He nodded at everyone, sat next to the city administrator, and said, "I need more money for overtime pay for that rally. The mayor can't expect my officers to work for free. I don't care who's coming to town."

An older woman with curly gray hair popped into the doorway. "Got a call from the Cheyenne Tribal rep. Her mother is sick, so she won't be able to attend today's meeting." And then she disappeared. Was she a supernatural, too? Zena wondered. Or only super stealthy?

A mid-sixties, short, stocky, barrel-chested man with raised scars striping the right side of his face from his chin to his scalp strutted into the room, a whiff of smoke trailing him. Wearing a cowboy hat, shirt, and denim jacket, he looked like the star of a Western. *Hero or villain?* His dark, narrow eyes darted around the room as if searching for someone. His gaze slid over Zena without even a nod and rested on Reid who looked anxious, maybe even a little afraid.

"Chairman Redhawk, so glad you can be here today," Reid said. "Can we offer you some coffee—"

The man's chest puffed up, and he bellowed, "Guess the mayor didn't think this was an important enough event for him to deign to attend. Sent his money man, instead."

Reid's face flushed. "Mayor Thompson will be stopping in later. He had a scheduling conflict. Conference call with the Governor."

The Chairman harrumphed and crossed his arms over his barrel chest. "Supporting the pipeline owners? They're the *real* problem. Profit over people."

He's in quick getaway mode, Zena noted. Come in, put people on the defensive, leave in a huff. She admired his chutzpah. *Today's winner of the pissing contest?*

Where was Jacob with those dreamy eyes? Heat rushed to her face and something coiled in stomach— and below. *Not now. No. He's off limits and no. No.*

Jacob hurried in. "Sorry I'm late. Hey, Uncle Dan. Glad you can be here."

Uncle Dan? Well, well, well, well, well. Was everyone related to everyone else in this town?

"There you are." Chairman Daniel embraced Jacob. "The most important member of this group has arrived."

"Ah, no." Jacob laughed, "That would be you."

At last, Chairman Dan sat and patted the space at the table next to him. "Saved a seat for you."

Jacob grinned at his uncle, and Zena's heart flipflopped. Jacob and his uncle clearly had a special relationship. The curmudgeon had a soft spot for Jacob and wasn't afraid to let it be seen. Unlike the snooty

Adalwolf family, this clan showed their emotions. *That's a refreshing change.*

Reid cleared his throat, and Jacob plopped into the chair next to his uncle. The man with his eye color that changed from hazel to quicksilver caught Zena staring at him as if he was a huckleberry cobbler. *Damn.* She nodded at him and gulped the remains of her java. *It's the caffeine jitters, nothing more.* Her traitorous thighs trembled in response, and she suppressed a groan.

"I'd like to go around the table and have everyone introduce themselves. I'll start." Keeping it brief, Reid introduced himself, referenced the mayor's scheduling conflict, and assured the group that he was there to support the efforts.

Hal Wiley was next, then Chairman Daniel, who raised his hands in wide gestures as he spoke, as if encouraging an audience to clap, then Jacob, and finally it was Zena's turn.

"I'm Special Agent Zena Adalwolf. I work with the Indian Country Crimes Unit, the ICCU, and I recently completed my on-the-ground training in New Mexico with the BIA, the FBI, and the DOJ."

Chairman Daniel barked, "Who do you think you are to come here and tell us what to do?"

Jacob placed his hand on his uncle's arm and said something she couldn't understand.

Keeping an even tone, she responded, "I'm here to assist this proactive taskforce in determining what obstacles exist in your ability to track missing and murdered Indian women."

"You're no older than a minute—"

She kept talking. He was not going to bulldoze her. She'd been invited to join this taskforce, and she was going to show him why she was valuable to this group.

"Most of the crimes in Indian Country are judged by the local tribal justice systems. The FBI's focus is on crimes of violence—murder, child sexual and physical abuse, sexual abuse of adults, human trafficking, and violent assault. We arrive *only* after a request from our tribal and Bureau of Indian Affairs and Office of Justice Services partners. The process requires collaboration and teamwork." She stood and gathered her things. "But it appears that won't happen here. It's clear I'm not welcome."

Chaos erupted and Jacob slammed his hand on the table. "My uncle wishes to say something to you." He glared at the older man. "Don't you?"

"I'm sorry," Chairman Daniel said with a sullen expression like a chastened child. "I didn't mean to suggest you didn't *know* what you were doing." He nodded at Jacob. "He thinks you have a good reason to be here. This, this *lecture*? That's bureaucrat-speak, mumbo-jumbo. I have a *personal* question for you."

She steeled herself. *Remain calm, do not allow him to bully you.*

"Everyone on the Crow rez—hell, every Indian in the U.S. and Canada has a family member or friend who's gone missing or been murdered." His eyes bore a hole into her head. "You don't understand the pain we suffer. Why should we trust you?"

"Five years ago, three of my sisters went out for a hike." Fighting emotion, holding herself in check, even though grief clawed at her chest like a trapped animal, she pushed on. "One was found with her throat slashed—nearly decapitated. The other two were raped and died as a result of their injuries." She tapped her index finger on the table with each word as her gaze swept the room. "This. Is. Personal."

****

Jacob wished she'd been able to keep this horrific story to herself, but his uncle pushed her to the brink and there was no holding her back. *Zena Adalwolf was magnificent.* With her green eyes blazing, spine ramrod straight, her face lit up with passion, Zena's strength and integrity had aroused him as no other woman ever had. Her scent was sweet and heady, and he struggled against the urge to leap across the table and carry her out of the hostile space.

Hostility caused by my uncle. Why did he have to behave like a bully? He'd always acted like a martyr and beat down others who opposed him. His winningest strategy was browbeating people and being ungracious in victory. At times, his aggressive nature was simply abusive.

Hal distributed an agenda and described the need for the taskforce. "As you are aware, in 1978, the United States Supreme Court removed tribal criminal jurisdiction over non-Indians. The DOJ has documented that most violent crimes against Native women are committed by non-Indians, white men in particular. Tribal governments are unable to bring charges against these perpetrators—when they can find them. As Chairman Redhawk has noted, the growing presence of the oil and gas industry has created a surge of non-Native males in the area—and increasing numbers of missing and murdered Native women.

"Unlike the epidemic on the Crow and Cheyenne reservations, Billings and Yellowstone County has not yet experienced the tragic impact of this industry. As much as many of us would like to prevent this from coming to Billings, there is no guarantee we can stop it from happening. All the more reason for us to put a plan together, beginning with some basic data."

The Billings chief of police distributed handouts with graphs and tables providing an overview of the city's violent crimes. Aggravated assaults led the statistics, followed by robbery, then rape. Only four criminal homicides. "We are seeing an uptick of incidents in some of our beats—Downtown, East, North Central, and Southwest. Last year there were only four criminal homicides." He nodded at Zena. "We called the FBI for help with about thirty cases. Mostly technical assistance."

Special Agent Adalwolf had taken everyone in that room by surprise. *A true warrior woman.* She took no prisoners—even at the risk of opening herself up to unthinkable pain. When he'd called Bert for info on the tiny FBI agent, the director of the black ops division told him what had happened in West Virginia. By *chance*, Zena had escaped her sisters' fate. He'd been blown away. He knew what she'd suffered. His father's decades old unsolved murder haunted him. Dreams about that fateful night woke him up in cold sweat, taunting him, leaving him shaken for hours, but not recalling the specifics of the nightmares. He was almost resolved to never being able to solve the cold case. *Almost.*

"What do you think, Jacob?" Hal asked.

Whoops. Caught daydreaming.

"I'm sure Jacob has better things to do than to take me out on a ride along on the reservation," Zena said with a hint of a smile. "Not that I wouldn't *like* to get to know the community better. Chairman Redhawk has correctly identified my lack of local tribal experience. Since the chairman knows everyone in the tribe and all the politics, maybe *he'd* like to take me around?"

"And be your *scout*?" Jacob's uncle snorted and shook his head. "I don't think so."

Jacob leaped into the budding conflict. "Great idea. When do you want to get started, Zena?"

"I'm on a short time frame, so the sooner I can get up to speed, the better."

Jacob's cell phone reverberated, the ring tone as loud as a fire horn in the quiet meeting room.

He stepped outside into the hallway.

"Graywolf."

"Jacob." His mother's voice hitched. "Your father. He came to see me at work—I was with a patient. He was covered in blood again. There's been another murder."

"Mom, calm down. Coral died of natural causes. No foul play." His mother's psychic powers—her healing power and her connections with animals and spirits—had always been well under her control. A vision while at work? *Is she losing it?* She wasn't that old. Not even sixty yet. Could she be showing the initial signs of dementia? As soon as the idea entered his mind, shame heated his face and guilt clawed at his chest. How could he think such a thing? There had to be some other explanation. "I'm sure I'll get a call if there's—" His phone beeped, and his heart sank. "Mom, I've got to go. Love you."

The female dispatcher's words poured out in a frantic rush. "Boss, you've got to get to Bighorn Canyon. Some hikers found a dead woman. Your friend, Ranger McGregor, called it in. Said she thinks she might be a member of our tribe."

His stomach dropped as if he'd been flipped on a rollercoaster loop-the-loop. "Tell them to stay put."

"They're all waiting for you. I'm texting the GPS coordinates from their satellite phone now."

Jacob stepped back into the conference room. "I'm sorry, everyone. There's been an incident." He nodded at Zena. "Your ride along starts now. It's a long trip to this site, over ninety miles. I suggest you take advantage of the City Hall rest rooms."

She pulled her things together and hurried to the hallway. "Do we have time to grab some water and take-out food? I get sick when I don't eat. Fast metabolism."

He quirked a smile. "Me, too. Meet me in the coffee shop across the street. I'll grab some sandwiches and drinks."

A little while later, a large brown paper bag in hand, Jacob ushered her into his patrol car. "Mind your head."

"Thanks for not pushing down on it as I got in." She laughed. "And for not putting me in the back seat."

"The cage is no place for a guest." He turned the key in the ignition. "We have a long trip ahead of us— maybe we could get to know each other better. You know, a trust-building exercise for new team members."

Sipping from her fresh coffee, she gave him the side eye. "Like what?"

Jacob pulled onto the Interstate and headed toward Hardin. "How about two lies and a truth?"

"Sure, but you have to pinky swear to keep

secrets." She put her little finger up. "Otherwise, no dice."

"Pinky swear." He laughed. "My mother is the only person who uses that. I prefer a blood oath."

She looked appalled. "You're joking."

"Well, I am an Indian." He smirked. "And yes, I'm kidding."

When he linked his pinky with hers, a sharp intake of breath took him by surprise. His not hers. He hoped she didn't see the effect she had on him. Zena's eyes sparkled with mischief. *Of course, she'd noticed.*

"Ready?" Perhaps she'd forget that awkward moment? *Not a chance.*

"I'll start." She turned in her seat to face him, the seatbelt straining at her full breasts. "One, I was an Olympic level gymnast. Two, my uncle is the richest man in West Virginia. Three, I'm a wolf shifter—a werewolf."

He cleared his throat. "Okay, let me see. You're petite enough to have been a gymnast, but I think the Olympic level is an exaggeration, even a lie. The owner of one of the biggest online retail sites lives in West Virginia. Unless your uncle has expanded from the winery, I think that's a lie also. So, that only leaves…wolf shifter as truth?"

"Like *you*," she said and poked him in the arm. "That's *your* truth."

He gulped. Other than his mother, no woman had ever known this before. Here she was, bold as brass, calling him out. "How'd you know?"

"Miriam gave me the clue before you even walked into the lobby at the Hotel LaBelle. But when you shook my hand." She cocked an eyebrow. "I knew.

Like calls to like, Jacob. The real question is, what do we do about it?"

Chapter Five

Crow Indian Health Service ~*~ Crow Agency, Montana

Trembling, Esther stumbled into the break room, dropped into a chair, and put her head in her hands. *Not again. Dear God, not again. And here at work. The visions were getting worse.* Joseph was bloodier this time. The last time, at home, the crimson was only on his head. This time, it dripped down to his neck, as if a bottomless wound kept oozing blood.

Brett and Robert came into the break room, chatting about the national parks in Montana.

"I was thinking of going hiking in Bighorn Canyon," Robert said, "but that would require good walking shoes and motivation—Esther? What's wrong?"

She glanced up, but their faces were blurred through her tears. "Oh. Just a bad day. I'll be okay."

"You're holding your temples like you have a migraine," Brett said. "Would you like something for pain?"

Shaking her head, she said, "Not sure that would help *this* headache."

Brett pulled a packet out of his pocket. "This is amazing stuff. Powdered aspirin, acetaminophen, and caffeine. Dissolves faster and goes straight to work."

"Hey." Robert nodded. "I use powdered pain relievers, too, but without the caffeine." He pulled a similar pouch out of his pocket. "Take this. You won't get the jitters."

"Hah." Brett raised his eyebrows. "Didn't know they made that without the jump juice. Thanks for the tip."

Esther accepted the meds from both men and stood. "Thanks, guys. Tell you what I'm going to do. It's lunchtime. I'm sure we have an empty exam room. I'm going to have a little lie down and put some cold water on my face." She gave a mirthless laugh. "I don't want to scare the patients."

Robert patted her on the shoulder and nodded. "Good idea. I'll be your lookout."

"Not necessary. I'll put out the in-use flag. No biggie. It's been done before."

He looked so abashed, Esther told him, "Don't worry, you'll get the hang of how we do things here."

Grabbing a wet paper towel and some ice cubes, she beelined to the space she'd evacuated in a panic. *Please don't be there, please don't be there, please don't be there—*

He stood in the corner as if waiting for her return. She sighed. "Joseph. I wish you could speak to me, sign to me, do anything other than materialize looking mortally wounded."

Only his eyes moved, tracking her pacing from one side of the room to the other.

"I called our son. Told him." She threw her hands up in the air. "What else do you want me to do? I'm a midwife, a healer, not a cop." Stopping in front of the apparition, she said in a softer voice. "I miss you so much. Part of me loves it when you visit—but not like this. Right after you died, you sat on the foot of our bed every night for a week, watching me. I'd wake up and see you there and think, *Thank God, he's not dead!* Then you'd shimmer away, and I'd remember you were gone. Murdered. Our son the only witness—who can't recall a thing about that night."

Did his face change? Or was it her imagination placing a sad expression on him, reflecting her sorrow, not his?

Esther clutched her chest, wishing she could hold him again, croon funny songs in his ear. For almost two decades, they'd had the best marriage. She would never love another man like she had Joseph. Even with Joseph coming to see them every day for over a year, it could never make up for not being able to truly be with the man she still loved.

"Remember how we met? My God, you were so tall and handsome with your long black hair. Your eyes! Like mercury, shifting color with your moods, pulling me in. In that black cowboy hat with the beaded band and those boots—well, you were imposing. You were the *Chief of the Crow Nation*. I confess, I was afraid of you when you showed up at the first aid tent at the fair. I feared you were coming there to give us a hard time, to yell at us." Closing her eyes, she hugged herself and rocked back and forth at the memory.

"Silly me. You thanked us for taking good care of your tribe. I was speechless, let my boss do all the talking. Me. Speechless." She guffawed. "I bet there were times you wished I'd stayed that way."

Sliding onto the exam table, she stared upward. Her beloved husband hovered over her out of reach. "I cried so hard my chest hurt. I cried for you. Then for our son. That night, after I found you—" her voice hitched and lowered to a whisper "—Jacob was huddled under the bushes, a terrified expression on his face, weeping softly, as if not to be heard."

She put the wet paper towel on her eyes. "Our boy, our sweet gift, our late in life child miracle baby. Traumatized so badly he couldn't speak for months. Elective mutism, the first psychiatrist said with that haughty, condescending air. *Common among Native Americans.* No, I told him, he has post-traumatic stress disorder. I found another doctor, someone who specialized in PTSD in children who witness violence." She paused. "Did I ever tell you what the first psychiatrist wrote on Jacob's chart? *Mother is aggressive bitch.* Me. A nurse midwife with years of experience whose husband was murdered and her son's spark snuffed out, his mind retreating further from me each day—I was a *bitch.* Bet he never imagined I'd see that file. I wrote him a thank you note, enclosing a copy of the page from the chart, of course. I told him I will *always* be my child's advocate. You should consider being one for your patients instead of disrespecting them and their culture."

A tap at the door silenced her monologue. "Yes?"

"Hey," Mary Longbow called out. "I'm back from lunch. The guys told me you didn't feel well."

Esther wiped her face with the towel. "I'm better, thanks, I'll be right out."

"Frances Deerfoot is here with contractions two minutes apart."

"This is her third child." Esther snatched open the door. "We don't have time to get her to the hospital floor. Bring her in here right now."

Mary raced into the room with Frances in a wheelchair while Esther grabbed blankets, trays of instruments, and other supplies. She yelled, "Someone call obstetrics, tell them we need a pick-up for a mother and child."

Hunched over and clutching her belly, the woman moaned, "Sorry to bother you."

Esther helped her onto the table and yanked out the stirrups. "Bother me? I *live* for this." *Hours of boredom, interspersed with moments of terror.* "Now let's bring this baby into the world so you can hold him or her to your heart forever."

****

The Doctor gazed into the waiting room filled with snotty kids, women who enjoyed being abused, and men who used meth to escape their hopeless lives. When they entered the exam room for their visits, it was almost *worshipful* the way their brown eyes admired him. Babies, so many babies. *Ugh.* At least he didn't have to deal with them. The midwife handled all of that lot. Esther. She was interesting. Pretty woman. Long black hair. Too bad she always kept it pulled back in a ponytail. A little old for his taste, but attractive. Not Asian. Not Indian, despite those high cheekbones. He'd bet his measly paycheck on that. Eastern European? That must be it. *She should be careful about who she pisses off. Even if her son is a cop, no one is immune from accidents.*

A timid tap at the door. "Doctor?" That stupid cow, Mary, stuck her face into the room. "There's someone to see you at the front desk." He resisted the urge to snarl at the lowly woman. He, after all, was a physician and more than worthy to be called Doctor with a capital D.

****

Bighorn National Recreation Area, Montana

As the car climbed through the mountainous region, Zena took a deep breath and pressed her hand to her aching heart. "I'm so sorry about your father, Jacob. No one can truly understand what it's like to have a loved one ripped out of your life by murder—at least I had some closure. The killer was captured and killed." She reached out and grasped his hand. "You can't remember *anything*?"

He shook his head. "Half a year of my life is gone from my memory. I remember being excited that my dad and I were going for a special midnight run together for my ninth birthday. My mother teased that it was the weirdest birthday party she'd ever heard of. Then she gave each of us a hug and said, 'See you in the morning.' That's the last thing I can recall from that night."

"And your mother's—cool with the whole shifter thing?"

"Mom has her own, shall we say, differences?" He quirked an eyebrow. "She's a healer."

"Of course, she is, she's a nurse." That's not supernatural," Zena said.

"What if I told you that when she places her hands on wounds they heal better and faster?" He smiled. "Don't look so skeptical. Not just humans. Animals, too. When I was little, I brought home a great horned owl with a broken wing. My father wanted nothing to do with him. My mother healed Tiger, and he still lives on our property, *his* territory." He told her about Eddy's

53

visit and Tiger swooping down at him—and his mother's ministrations. "Great horned owls are tigers of the sky. The kid got off lucky with a few scratches. People have been maimed by those feathered predators."

"Remind me not to piss him off," Zena said, and shook her head. "So, is he like your mother's familiar?"

"Not exactly, but they are good friends." He gave her a sideways glance. "One more thing."

She gripped the door handle. "Should I brace myself?"

"Depends on how you feel about ghosts," he said. "I can't see them, but my mother does."

"Is that all you've got? That's it?" Zena released a shaky laugh. "Have you been to the Hotel LaBelle lately? Spook central."

He chuckled. "Well, there is that."

"Does it happen a lot, her seeing ghosts?"

"Right after my father was killed, she said he visited her every night for a year. After that, he only showed up for their anniversary."

Dead and gone, but still loving his wife enough to show up on their special day. Half to herself she murmured, "What a romantic guy."

"He was, actually. Always brought her flowers on Fridays. Would dance her around the kitchen and tell her she was the sun to his moon." A hint of nostalgia entered his voice. "I wish his visits were only to dance now."

"What do you mean?"

"Lately he's been showing up dripping in blood."

A shudder ran down Zena's spine. "When was his last visit?"

He sighed. "My mother saw him today."

Her stomach lurched in free fall. "The first call you took? That was your mother?"

He nodded. "She told me my father showed up at the clinic."

She gasped. "My God, Jacob, what a terrible burden for her."

"The last time he showed up, Eddy's mother died. My mother said she was murdered. The ME said natural causes, a heart attack."

Her mind reeling, Zena could only imagine the stress his mother was experiencing. Her husband dies, then reappears to warn her when others die? "And today? The same thing?"

"Honestly, I don't know what to think anymore. She's not that old, but the job is wearing her down. Thirty years of delivering babies in a medical outpost could get to a person, even one as dedicated as my mother." He pulled into Bighorn Canyon National Park with his lights flashing. "She's claiming it's murder—again."

Jacob steered the SUV slowly down the embankment. The beauty of the park took Zena's breath away, momentarily distracting her from the reason for their journey. Azure water sparkled before them. A small scattering of RVs, tents, and teepees hugged the shores of the bay, thin trails of smoke curling into the clear mid-October sky. With the temperature in the mid-thirties, she was grateful she'd grabbed her down jacket that morning.

"I'm surprised to see this many campers out here. It must have been freezing last night. Isn't there a storm warning for this week, too?"

"It's a year-round camp site," Jacob responded. "Hard core outdoorsmen and women prefer this time of year. No tourists."

"I can appreciate that. My hometown is jammed with tourists three out of four seasons. Local businesses love to see them come, but the residents love to see them go."

He pulled the vehicle alongside a park ranger's truck. Yellow tape flapped in the breeze, and a cluster of people stood around the perimeter. "Maybe we'll get lucky and have some witnesses."

A tall, athletic woman, clad in a brown and beige ranger uniform, bearing a badge and a side arm, waved to them. Zena climbed out of the passenger side and waited for Jacob to do the introductions.

"Ranger McGregor, this is FBI Special Agent Zena Adalwolf. She's in Billings working on an interagency taskforce with me. I asked her to come along."

She nodded at Zena. "Good timing. You outrank me and this guy. I'm happy to hand this over to you." She pointed to a young couple huddled against each other on the sidelines of the enforced perimeter, the girl's face streaked with tears. "These folks found her. Called 9-1-1 and park services right away. Thank God they have a satellite phone."

Zena wanted a closer look at the body under the multicolored blanket next to a teepee, but she'd circle back to that task. "Did you get photos of the scene before you covered the victim, Ranger McGregor?"

"Yes, ma'am." She pulled out her phone and handed it to Zena. "Jacob, I think she might be one of yours."

Jacob looked over Zena's shoulder as she scrolled

through the array of pictures, his warm breath tickling her ear. "She looks like she fell asleep," Zena observed. "Odd position, though."

"Witnesses told me she'd been chatting with them the night before, told them she wanted a little time away for herself. Been having some personal issues. Nothing specific."

The ranger shook her head. "This morning they came over to ask her if she wanted some coffee. Found her like this." She lowered her voice. "If I were a betting gal, I'd put my money on suicide."

"That's up to the medical examiner," Zena said. "We give them the facts and go from there, right Jacob?"

His face was the color of bleached bones.

"Jacob." Zena grabbed his arm. "What's wrong?"

"I know her. We've been friends since we were kids. It's Skye Martinez. She works at the Tribal Council Office, distributes the monthly checks." He passed his hand over his face. "Husband left her last week."

"I can handle this." Zena pulled a pair of black nitrile gloves out of her pocket. "This is your friend. Take a breath."

Jacob nodded, his face a mask of sorrow. "Her mother will be devastated." He climbed inside the SUV and grabbed the transmitter.

"Ranger McGregor, could you take the names, addresses, and phone numbers of all these potential witnesses for us, please?"

The blonde pulled out a notepad and pen. "You got it."

Zena took more photos of the scene from different

angles, then stepped into the crime scene. She turned around in a circle, snapping panoramic shots of entrance and egress, making sure she included the sparkling bay. Poking her head into the teepee, she noted a sleeping bag, a leather tote bag, three grocery store bags, and a case of bottled water. *Looked like she was planning to stay a few days.* After more photos, she stepped inside—moving around the personal items with care. Nothing leaped out at her as being out of place. She'd let the CSI team inventory every gum wrapper and piece of lint. Not her favorite part of an investigation.

When she emerged from the unoccupied teepee, the crowd had moved away. Ranger McGregor stalked from person to person taking notes. She reminded Zena of her high school principal. Intimidating, but caring.

Taking a deep breath, Zena squatted next to the blanket and removed it with caution, not wanting to disturb any type of smaller evidence. The woman's spine was contorted, and her long black hair pooled around her head, exposing her high forehead and temples. Her wide-open eyes stared back at Zena, unseeing. A dried up trickle of blood ran from behind the victim's ear down her neck. Jacob needed to see this. A frothy clot of white matter sat on her blue lips. The fingers of her right hand curled in, clutching at her chest. Moving to the other side, Zena noted the woman's left hand still held a water bottle. *That she would bag and take with her.*

"Jacob," she called. "You might want to see this."

He drew closer to the scene appearing more composed. "What did you find?"

"I've seen photos of people who've died like this.

Same arched back, same foam at the mouth." She glanced up. "We'll need a tox screen to be sure, but it looks like strychnine poisoning."

From behind Jacob, the ranger chimed in on the last part of the conversation. "It's in gopher and mole pellets, available at every garden supply shop in the area. We try to educate folks about using non-toxic controls for pests, but not everyone is patient enough to try something different. Usually it's the family pet that dies, not the owner."

"Horrible way to go," Jacob retorted.

Zena agreed. "There's one more thing." She pulled back the tip of the woman's left ear. "Do you happen to know if Skye had surgery recently?"

Chapter Six

Crow Indian Health Service ~*~ Crow Agency, Montana

Tears streaming down his cheeks, arms open for a hug, the old guy at the desk called him "son" and lunged. Almost tripping over his own feet in his haste to put space between them, the Doctor glanced around the room to see who was watching this spectacle unfold. A few rheumy-eyed gray-hairs sat in the waiting area. They seemed more intent on their own family drama than his. *Good.* He had to get this man out of here. *But how?*

"Hey, why don't we have this conversation in private." The space he shared with the other Doctor wouldn't work. But the administrator's office showed no light through the glass side panels. He tried the knob—it opened. Breathing a sigh of relief, he waved the wizened man into a chair and closed the door. "Have a seat, please. Tell me why you think we're related?"

The stranger picked at the sleeve of his ratty sweater, avoiding the Doctor's eyes. "DNA. The registry said we were a match. I ain't got no brothers, so I knew it could only be you."

"I'm sure there must be some mistake. I've never taken any DNA test—" *Medical school.* That researcher must have *sold* his blood samples. How else would someone have obtained his genetic material? The written informed consent form stated it was *anonymous, untraceable, results to be reported only in the aggregate, no individuals would ever be identified.* When the test came back negative for cancer risk, he'd been so relieved, he'd even thanked the researcher for allowing him to participate in the study. *The bastard.*

Saggy orange-tinged eyes fixed on the Doctor, the elder rasped, "I'm your pappy."

The Doctor appraised the stooped-over man with the swollen belly and jaundiced skin sitting before him. *He looks nothing like me.* An alcoholic, living in his vitamin deprived, wet brain fantasies. *He can take his raggedy ass out the front door and never come back.*

"Sorry. I don't see any family resemblance. There must be some mistake." The Doctor stood. "Hope you didn't have to travel far to receive this bad news."

"I'm sick. Pancreatic cancer. I had to find you before I died." The geezer gave him a beseeching look. "I want to put things right. Make amends." He reached into his back pocket and produced a billfold. Hands shaking, he removed a frayed photograph from the wallet and placed it on the keyboard in front of the Doctor. "You look like me when I was a young man, before the drink took me."

The room whirled, and the Doctor gripped the edge of the desk. Fury rose in his chest. If there hadn't been a piece of furniture between them, he would have struck the loser down without remorse. The bastard deserved to die in agony. Taking a deep breath, the Doctor ground the words out between his teeth, "No, there's no resemblance at all."

"Son—"

"Don't call me son," he shouted. Breathing like a bull chasing a red flag, he pointed at the door. "*Get out.* Get out before I call the security guard."

Using the arms of the chair to assist himself, the old man rose, unsteady on his feet. His face creased with bewilderment. "I don't understand. Why won't you talk to me?"

"Well, *Dad,* if you actually were my father, you'd know the answer to that, wouldn't you? You would know that you abandoned me and left me to be abused in one foster home after another. Where were you when the bigger boys were beating me and burning me with cigarettes? Why didn't you come rescue me when the foster parents decided they were tired of me? How about when I was raped—*repeatedly*—in a state-run group home I didn't belong in?"

Slack jawed, the old man's face crumpled, and tears began to stream down his face. "I'm sorry. I had no idea. I tried to find you. Your mother—"

The Doctor slammed his hand on the desk. "Bullshit!"

The diseased creature, his so-called *father*, stumbled backward, eyes filled with fear. "I'm sorry, I'm sorry—" Sobbing, he fled the room.

The Doctor sank into the chair and scrubbed his face with his hands. How dare that despicable piece of human waste show up at his place of work. Things were coming together for him, finally. How dare that bastard try to ruin his life—*again*? He glanced at the fading color photo on the desk and jumped. Not three, but *four* smiling faces stared back at him.

****

Billings City Hall

At Jacob's urging, Hal Wiley convened an emergency session of the Interagency Task Force, minus the city administrator who was on vacation. This time Tommy Otterlegs and Mayor Wells joined them in the conference room—their expressions as dark as the clouds outside.

Police Chief James began the meeting. "Only four homicides in the City of Billings last year. We don't know if the latest death is a murder. We haven't even heard back from the ME. Aren't we jumping the gun?"

"I hear you." Jacob nodded. "But Zena and I were at the scene—there was something *off* about it. I've asked Joe to rush the autopsy." He glanced at Tommy. "Plus, Tommy has a case he wants to discuss."

Jacob's heart went out to the guy. His sister's death had hit him hard, and he'd been unable to appease his wife, Wanda, about his naughty nephew. The grandmother now had Eddy in her house. A decision, Tommy had told Jacob, that would keep him up at night.

A subdued version of the old bantam rooster now spoke. "Last June, the body of a middle-aged woman was discovered in a vehicle in the Cheap Eats parking lot. When the woman did not respond to knocks on the window, the store employee called 9-1-1. The officer on the scene noted that it appeared she had fallen asleep after shopping. Her trunk was full of groceries and a receipt was in her purse with a time stamp."

"That place is always busy," the mayor interrupted. "Why would the employee think something was wrong?"

"She recalled the car being there the previous day,

recognized the bumper stickers. Said it was odd it was still there."

"Don't they have surveillance cameras?"

"Yes," Tommy responded. "The car was parked away from the store, but the videos showed the woman placing her bags in the trunk of the car. She went around the vehicle and that was the last she was seen on camera. She was found in the driver's seat—her head lying back on the head rest. The ME said she died from a heart attack."

The mayor's brow furrowed. "So, natural causes, yes?"

"Maybe. The woman, Kimani Fleetfoot, was a member of the Shoshone Tribe. When these new cases—" his voice cracked "—occurred, it reminded me of this one, and I asked the ME for a copy of his files."

"And?" the mayor growled.

"Buried on page ten of the report, the ME noted a wound at the base of her scalp."

Mayor Wells threw his hands up. "Are we playing twenty questions? Can someone tell me what the hell this means?"

Jacob cleared his throat. "This is the third Native American woman who has died under unusual circumstances"

"You said," the mayor argued, "they died of heart attacks. A *lot* of people die of heart disease. I had stents put into my heart two years ago because I had clogged arteries. How is this uncommon? If I remember correctly from the city's Healthy Heart event in February, Native Americans are more likely to have heart disease—and to die from its causes."

"Yes," Jacob replied, attempting to control the

annoyance in his voice. "But usually people who die of heart attacks *don't* have fresh scars on their scalps."

The Mayor drummed his fingers on the table. "How many are we talking about?"

"Three," Jacob said. "Zena, could you please explain what this means?"

She nodded. "Gentlemen, we may be dealing with a serial killer."

"Now wait a minute," the mayor exploded. "That can't be true. We're *only* talking about three women—"

Chairman Redhawk jumped to his feet. "Only? Did you say *only* three women? Is that because they're Indians, so their deaths don't matter? Would it matter if they were *white*?"

"No. No. You completely misunderstood me," the mayor backpedaled. "There needs to be more—"

Redhawk slammed his hand on the table. "No more dead women. Isn't that why we have this taskforce, to prevent deaths of more Indian women?"

"Yes, but, a serial killer—that's insane. We're a nice little city, America's hometown. You start using that term and no one will want to visit—and some might even move away."

"The number is only part of the reason why I'm stating this," Zena said. "There is a *pattern*. The women are all Native American. All died of what appeared to have been a heart attack. And all had scars along their hairlines."

"Someone is scalping the Indians," Redhawk chuffed in a mirthless laugh. "Very old school."

"That is *not* what she said, Uncle Dan," Jacob corrected. "We are putting the key pieces on the table for everyone in this task force to show you the patterns and to raise our concerns. Isn't that why we're all here?"

The room fell silent for a few beats. Jacob gave each person an assessing look, wondering if police work or politics would prevail.

"What do you want from me?" Chief James asked.

Relief flooded Jacob's chest. The police chief had been the fish he wanted to catch. "We need to create a timeline. If you could provide us with a list of cases that might fit this pattern, that would be a great help. Saint Vic's and the local funeral directors would fall under your jurisdiction. Could your office handle those queries, too?"

Chief James nodded. "I'm going to need more money, but yeah, we can do that. I'll pass on whatever looks promising to you and Special Agent Adalwolf."

A subtle smile, quick to disappear, appeared on Zena's lips. She'd been accepted by the police chief. Jacob marveled at her ability to remain professional while within the belly of the old boys' club. Had their roles been reversed, Jacob knew he wouldn't be nearly as gracious as the agent.

"This has to be kept under wraps," the mayor grumbled. "The last thing we need is panicked citizens."

"You're absolutely correct, mayor," Jacob said with more than necessary deference to mollify the politician. "As always, our response should be *We cannot discuss an ongoing investigation.*"

"And we don't want our unsub to know we have spotted a pattern," Zena interjected. "The perpetrator could be anyone, even—" she paused "—someone we know."

Chapter Seven

Crow Indian Health Service ~*~ Crow Agency, Montana

As Esther headed for the clinic's exit at the end of a long day thinking about a long hot soak in the tub, a kid bounded up to her like an excited puppy.

"Hey, Auntie Esther," Eddy exclaimed. "I was wondering if I'd see you."

"This is my other home," she responded with a wave around the primary care clinic. "What brings you here?"

Hop-walking, as if preparing for the Crow Fair dance competition, he said, "I saw Dr. Bob."

She had to think for a moment. "Oh, Dr. Mann."

"Yeah, he said it was okay to call him Dr. Bob." Eddy leaped at the doors which opened automatically. "I like him—he's nice."

"That's good." She wished she had half this kid's energy. The wind whistled around the corner of the building, cutting through her down jacket. Eddy wore only a zip up hoodie—and it flapped open in the wind. "Did you get a shot?"

Dribbling an invisible basketball, Eddy bounded into the air. "Swish! And he scores!" He grinned. "No shots this time. A check-up."

"Everything okay?" *Where did I leave my car? It's*

not that big a parking lot.

Another dribble, another score. "He said I was too skinny." He shot her a side look. "I need to eat more pot roast."

She laughed. "Did he also prescribe more challah?"

"That bread?" He rubbed his stomach and licked his lips. "Yes, yes, that's exactly what he said."

"Doesn't your grandmother feed you?"

He stopped twirling. "She does—but she doesn't have a lot—and I'm *always* hungry."

Esther placed her hand on his shoulder. "Eddy, does your grandmother need help? We can ask Chairman Dan—"

His big brown eyes widened. "No, please don't. She'd be embarrassed." He lowered his voice. "Besides, she doesn't like him and doesn't want to owe him anything."

Fiercely independent, Mrs. Otterlegs was not alone in that sentiment. Although he was elected chairman by a majority, rumors circulated that he had verbally twisted arms and forced people to vote for him.

Esther nodded. "I have some leftover brisket and challah. How about if I bring it to your house? Would that be okay?"

"Sure."

"Won't your grandmother be wondering where you are?" *Where was Mrs. Otterlegs?* He was a minor. An adult should have been with him at the clinic. The wind whipped at her face, and tears formed on her eyelashes. "Eddy, did you have an appointment with Dr. Mann?"

Looking down, he dragged his foot across the asphalt and played with the zipper on his woefully thin jacket. "He told me to drop in anytime I wanted to talk.

I had a bad day at school."

She grabbed his freezing cold hand. "We can talk in the car. Let's get you home."

"Can I come see Tiger?"

He gave her a beseeching look, one that reminded her of her son at that same age. Painful memories rose up, threatening to seize the present. She hurt for her son all over again, and now for Eddy.

"Your grandmother is going to be wondering where you are." She unlocked the door and pointed to the passenger seat. "Let's call her, okay?"

"All right." He shrugged. "But she's not home."

"Where is she?" *Lord, why are you testing me?*

"She's in the hospital," he said in a whisper. "Something to do with her heart."

"How long has she been in there? Who's looking after you?" No child, this one *in particular*, should be left alone at this time. He was putting up a brave front, but he must be terrified.

"A couple of days." He stared out the window. "I'm staying with Auntie Rose. She lives next door to my grandmother."

"Mrs. Elktooth?"

He nodded.

Rose Elktooth had six kids, a different father for each child, and an ongoing battle with meth. Jacob was there at least once a month on domestic violence calls—but Rose never showed up in court. She always took the man back. That was no place for Eddy.

"Would you like to visit your grandmother?"

His face brightened. "Yes, that would be great."

"Let's pick some flowers up at the gift shop. Is that okay with you?"

He nodded so hard his hair tumbled into his face.

"Good. Before we go, can we talk about what happened today?"

He traced a circle on the torn knee of his jeans. "Maybe."

"Was it those bullies again?" She wanted to storm the school, find those little schmucks, and yell at them. Dyslexia didn't mean he should be their verbal punching bag. "About reading?"

"They called me a foster kid and told me I'd wind up in jail, like my father."

She white-knuckled the steering wheel. "Where were the teachers when this was going on?"

"I dunno."

"First of all, you have a family. A *great* one." His father was in jail for involuntary manslaughter, that much was true. "Just because your dad's in jail doesn't mean you will be." She'd bet her challah that those bullies had a least one relative in jail at any given time.

"Did you know Dr. Bob was a foster kid?"

"That has never come up in our conversations."

"He said he was moved from foster home to foster home and even lived in a group home, but he did okay." Eddy gave her a sideways glance. "Dr. Bob said he got a lot of scholarships, that I should work hard, and maybe I could go to medical school, too."

"That would be wonderful. We need more doctors who understand Indian culture."

He sighed and ran his fingers through his hair. "I'm not smart enough."

Esther's heart caught in her throat. "Eddy, I never want to hear that from you again. You need some help with your reading, but other than that, you're very smart. You have a lot of talents other kids don't have."

He grinned. "Like stealing?"

She shook her head and laughed. "We are going to put your mind to better uses, my friend." Bracing herself for the freezing wind, she opened the car door. "Let's go see your grandmother."

****

Billings City Hall

As the rest of the participants left the conference room, Zena gathered up her things, acutely aware that Jacob had stayed behind and stood nearby. His scent transformed from all business to all pleasure, and her body responded to his call. Nipples hardening, her loins heating, she simultaneously welcomed his approach and loathed her keenness to mate with him. They hadn't even had a date, for Heaven's sake, and here she was fantasizing about pushing him up against the wall and climbing him like a tree.

"Want to go someplace for dinner?" His whisper caressed her neck, and a ripple of pleasure thrilled her. An urge to grab him nearly overcame her.

She turned and found herself inches away from his lips and other intriguing body parts. She arched a brow. "Only dinner?"

"For now." Jacob reached behind her, brushing her arm as he did so. A heady mixture of male and female sex pheromones wrapped her in an erotic embrace. "Don't forget your tablet."

"Thanks," she mumbled, her mouth dry. "Where do you have in mind?"

"It's a place one of my relatives owns. The food is good, and on the weekends the entertainment is great."

"Your car or mine?" She wanted to say your *place*

or mine but restrained her tongue.

"It's right here in town. Leave your SUV where it is. I'll bring you back to it later." He waved her out the door. "I can't wait for you to meet my cousin."

The blustery wind snuck under her coat, down her neck, and through her pants. "Brrr. Is it always this cold in October?"

"This is warm," he responded with a grin. "There's a saying, *Come to Montana for the scenery, stay because you can't start your car.*"

"Oh, that definitely makes me look forward to November." She climbed into the passenger seat of his cruiser. "What do you do in the winter for entertainment?"

His smile grew broader. "Indoor sports."

"Like basketball?" she teased.

The look in Jacob's eyes told her his mind wasn't on shooting hoops. *Maybe she should crack a window? Clear some of this pheromone fog?* No. She was enjoying it, and it appeared Jacob was too.

"That," he teased as he put the car in gear, "and some other games." He gave her a sly glance. "Ones that require enthusiasm and endurance."

"Why, Chief Graywolf. I do believe you're flirting with me."

"Would that be a bad thing?"

"No." A frisson of pleasure ran down her spine pushing away the cold. "It's a good thing, a very good thing." *Screw protocol.* This was the first guy she'd met in her life who was not a jerk, *was* a wolf shifter, and didn't treat her like damaged goods because she was different.

He pulled the vehicle into a spot in front of a two-story building. "Let's see where this goes, shall we?"

Here was a man who didn't speak to her in condescending tones because she wasn't one of the clan. What a refreshing change.

She grabbed his hand and squeezed. "I like you, Jacob. There are some things you need to know about me before we go too far. You might want to reconsider after I tell you."

"Way to lead me on." He squeezed back. "That makes me all the more intrigued."

"Don't say I didn't warn you."

"Duly noted." He climbed out of the car. "Deep, dark secrets make a delicious side dish."

Jacob led Zena into the dimly lit club, and a titan of a black-haired woman in a stylish black skirt, cobalt blue top, and wide red belt strode over to them, trailed by man dressed like Elvis.

"Welcome to the Garrett!" Then the woman exclaimed, "Jacob, is that you?" She placed her hand on her chest. "Oh, my God, it's been *forevah* since I've seen you." She gave Zena a once over. "And with a date, no less. To what do we owe this special occasion?"

"Zena," Jacob said, "this is my cousin Stephanie and her husband, Rod, aka Elvis."

Stephanie grabbed Zena in a bear hug, startling her. "Girl, you are cuter than a pixie! Where are you from? What brings you to Billings? How did you meet my handsome cousin?"

Overwhelmed with the welcome, Zena spoke through smushed lips, "If you let me go, I promise to tell you everything."

Releasing her captive, Stephanie laughed. "She's

funny, too! Where have you been all his life?"

"I'm from a little resort town in West Virginia, I'm here on temporary assignment with the FBI, and I'm on an interagency task force with Jacob." She paused. "Did I miss anything?"

Stephanie placed a well-manicured red-slick nail on her cheek. "You're leaving something out. What is it?"

Jacob spoke up, rescuing her. "We're hungry. It's been a long day. You can interrogate her after you feed us."

Stephanie led them through a buzzing dining room to a table for two in a quiet corner and handed them menus. "I recommend tonight's special, lamb chops and butternut squash. Do you want wine?"

"No," Zena responded. "I'm sensitive to alcohol. One drink and I'm out."

Stephanie chuckled. "Not to worry. We have lots of soft drinks." She headed toward the kitchen, and Elvis climbed the stage with a guitar in hand.

"Dinner and a show. Can't beat that," Zena said. "Your cousin is charming."

"She's a busybody," he warned. "Tell her one thing and it's out on the Indian telegraph the next day."

"Indian what?"

"Grapevine. It's faster than the Internet, trust me." He glanced around the room. "By tomorrow, everyone in Billings will know not only that we were here, but what we ate. There will also be rumors that we're getting married and someone will start planning a wedding feast."

"Hmm. Sounds like Summertown in reverse. Whenever I dated someone, the guy's buddies would tell him I was damaged goods and to steer clear of me."

He gave her a hard look. "Seriously?"

"Small town, small minds. According to some people, my Uncle Lowell included, I should have gone hiking with the other kids and none of that would have happened." She shook her head. "Like I don't feel enough survivor's guilt."

"That's horrible. If you'd gone with your sisters that day, you could have been another victim."

A hard edge of bitterness cut away at the pleasure of the evening. "They think I should have been the only victim—that the rest would have been spared if I'd gone. Because I'm different. I'm a red wolf and they're gray werewolves. In their minds, it was my *job* to be the scapegoat."

"I'm sorry. No one should be treated that way."

"Now you know my secret. I'm an outcast. Nobody wants me in Summertown—except my brothers and parents." She sighed. "My mother still believes I'll come home, marry a guy I dated one time in high school, and become the lawyer for the Adalwolf family business."

"Well, my mother—" His phone pinged as their food arrived. "Speaking of whom—" He put the cell to his ear. "Hi, Mom, what's up?"

His expression changed from playful to alarmed, and his face paled. "I'm on my way." He motioned to Stephanie. "We need to-go boxes."

Zena's heart rate kicked up three notches. "What's wrong?"

He shook his head at Zena, while his cousin rushed off. A bare two minutes later, he accepted the bag of food from Stephanie and hustled Zena out the door.

When they were in the cruiser, she repeated her question. "What's wrong?"

"My mother had another vision," Jacob spoke as he turned on the flashing bar lights. "And now another Indian woman is dead."

Chapter Eight

Crow Indian Health Service ~*~ Crow Agency, Montana

Jacob pulled the cruiser into the hospital driveway. Without a word, Zena leaped out of the vehicle after him and stayed on his heels. He found his mother sitting in the lobby with Eddy Little Bear. The kid was trying to keep up a good front, but his trembling chin, puffy eyes, and tear-streaked face belied his stoicism. His mother, appearing only slightly more together than the boy, sat with her arm wrapped around Eddy's shoulder searching the crowd as they entered the hospital. A look of relief crossed her face as soon as her gaze snagged his.

"Thank God you're here!" she exclaimed. "When it happened, we were tossed out of Mrs. Otterlegs' room, Tommy's on his way, and Eddy—" her voice hitched "—has been a real trouper."

Seeing his mother protecting another young boy sent him back to that terrible time in his life. A void in his memory, too traumatized to speak for six months, but he remembered her patient, enduring love. During that long, dark passage after his father's murder, she'd been at his side fighting for him every single day. She'd grasped onto him, never let him fall down into the permanent black hole of despair, all the while grieving her own loss. Now, the kid had the lioness at *his* side. She would hang onto Eddy during his valley of the shadow of death—and beyond.

In two strides, he was at his mother's side, pulling her and Eddy in for a group hug. "I'm so sorry," he husked. "I'm so very sorry."

Eddy began bawling and clung to him with all the strength his skinny arms could muster. "I—I have no place to go, she was my last real home, she loved me as much as my mom did, I don't know what to do—"

"It's okay, Eddy, we've got you." Jacob patted him on his back. Extricating himself from the tangle of arms, he turned to Zena and said, "Could you please take Eddy to a quiet spot while I speak with my mother?"

"Hey, Eddy." She crouched down to his level. "I'm Zena. I'm working with Chief Graywolf. Would you like to go to the chapel? Say a few prayers for your grandmother?"

Glassy-eyed, Eddy nodded, rose, and allowed Zena to steer him down the hall.

Jacob turned back to his mother. "What happened?"

"Eddy told me his grandmother was in the hospital. Heart problems." She pushed her long black hair away from her eyes. "We were in her room and she was so happy to see Eddy. He gave her some flowers—and she asked him to put them in the plastic water pitcher—and then she asked for her purse. I found it in the bottom drawer of her nightstand and handed it to her." His mother looked away. "I feel so responsible."

"Mom, you said it was her heart. How could you be responsible?"

Tears trickled down her cheek, she took a deep sobbing breath, and shrugged.

When she remained silent, he asked, "What happened next?"

"She took some money out of her bag and tried to give it to me. I said, no, it was my pleasure. She had a headache. I told her she should let the nurse know, so she could bring her something. She waved me off, said she didn't need to bother the nurses. She had her own medicine."

Her shoulders shook and Esther paused to catch her breath.

"She mixed it in a glass of water and took a sip—" Full on sobbing now, his mother struggled to speak. "She…smiled at us, smacked her lips—and then made a face like it was bitter. Next thing we knew she was having a seizure. I rang the call button, told the nurses we had an emergency, and pulled Eddy into the hall."

Jacob nodded. *Always protecting kids*.

"The STAT team arrived, and they closed the door. I don't know what they did. All I know is not five minutes after her seizure—" she lowered her voice to a whisper "—your father showed up, and this time the dripping blood was down to his arms."

Behind him a familiar voice boomed. "You're the person I want to talk to."

Jacob stood and faced his Uncle Daniel. "You know about Eddy's grandmother?"

He nodded once, an abrupt jerky movement. "Yes, I do. I was on my way to visit her when I got the message. What's this, the fourth woman?"

Jacob motioned for his uncle to keep his voice down. "We don't know the cause of death. She *was* in the hospital for heart disease. And my mother was there. She called for the code team."

Daniel sat down. "Esther, how are you holding up?" He reached for her hand, but she slid it away. "You know, I've been trying to reach you, but you haven't been returning my calls."

She spared Daniel a glance, then looked away. "I've been busy. No time for a social life."

"Your son's a man now," Daniel said with a smile. "You could use an evening out, maybe go to the Billings Club for dinner?"

"Not now, Daniel." Her lips thinned. "As you can see, I've got a few things on my plate."

Still smiling, the chairman nodded, but the scars on his face and neck swelled and reddened.

He'd been pursuing Jacob's mother for years, to no avail. As a kid, he'd believed it was because she didn't want to follow the old Indian tradition of a man marrying his brother's widow. As he grew older and learned more about grief, he believed she'd been in mourning, unable to give up her beloved Joseph. But today, in the stark light of the hospital lobby, he saw something he'd never noticed before—loathing.

****

Zena sat with her hands in her lap, absorbing the peace of the multi-faith chapel. Sunshine streamed through a large stained-glass window featuring a prominent white dove in flight holding an olive branch in its beak. Below the bird, azure blue waters churned, but the promise of a rainbow glittered above. She closed her eyes, and her mind went back to the funerals for her sisters in a similar space. Three lead-lined closed caskets, due to the radioactivity still present in their bodies, had been draped with white roses and placed on the stage in front of the mourners. As she had entered the funeral service, all heads turned toward her. One by one, recognition dawned, and the friendly glances turned to narrow-eyed glares. A chorus of whispers followed her to the front row where the immediate family waited. One message had resonated from that sibilant sound—*It should have been you, Coyote.* A cruel name to show she was different and should have been killed instead.

"You asleep, Miss Zena?" A child's voice broke into her painful memories, saving her from drowning in guilt.

"No, I'm meditating." She gazed at the boy—he was almost her height, and based on those high-water pants he was wearing, she guessed he was going through a growth spurt. A kid who had lost first his mother, and now his grandmother. Gangly adolescence and hormone hell awaited him, but right now, he was a scared little boy.

"Do you think my grandmother is with my mother?" His chin trembled. "I don't want them to be lonely."

Like he was right now.

Zena had given up on organized religion a long time ago. But she believed in the afterlife, and that loved ones never disappeared. Their energy remained long after their bodies were gone.

"I'm betting your grandmother and mother had a nice family reunion, and they're with other members of your tribe." She ran a finger through his hair, flipping it out of his eyes. *He's so earnest.*

"Are your mom and grandma dead, too?"

"No." She shook her head. "But I am familiar with the pain in your heart. I lost my three sisters a few years ago. There is a hole in my life that no one else will ever fill. I do know that as long I remember them, they live on."

He gulped and a lone tear trickled down his cheek. "I want to hug them and tell them I love them."

"You can do that anytime, anywhere." She put her arm around his shoulder. "Call out to them and say, 'I love you and I miss you.' You can ask them to send you a sign."

His brow furrowed. "I don't understand?"

"I was truly close to my sisters. We did everything together until I went to college. When we wanted to talk, we'd send an email or text with our favorite song." Her vision blurred. "When I need to hear from my sisters, I ask them to send our song."

"And it works?"

She gave a shaky laugh. "Yes. I turn on the radio, or walk into a diner, or my phone rings—and there's our song"

"Wow." He nodded. "We didn't have a favorite song, but my mother and grandmother were trying to teach me how to bead. I wasn't any good. If I ask them to send me a sign, do you think they'll send me beads?"

"That's up to them to decide. You'll recognize it when their gift arrives."

He leaned against her and looked up. "That window is pretty. It makes me feel peaceful."

"Me, too." Zena gazed at the dove, wondering if the glint in its eye was new, or had it been there all along and she hadn't seen it.

"Auntie Esther sent me in to see Grandmother, told

me we should have some special time together." He sighed. "When I was with Grandma. she made me feel the same way. Calm, no worries. She told me she had a visitor earlier that day, one of the doctors from the clinic. He told her he needed to do something—it would help her. She said he was nice."

Zena's skin began to prickle, and she tried to keep her voice even. "What did he do?"

He bent his head, lifted his hair, and pointed at the base of his scalp. "He said he had to take a boppsy from here."

An alarm bell rang in her head. "A biopsy?"

"Yeah, that's what it was." He sat up. "She said it didn't even hurt, he numbed it up good."

Her breath caught in her throat. "Did she say which doctor it was?"

"Nah. She said he was one of the nice ones." He wriggled in his seat. "They're all nice, but I especially like Dr. Bob. Do you think he came to visit my grandma?"

"I don't know, Eddy," she said, trying to restrain the thrill that ran through her muscles, calling her to the hunt, "but I'm sure we'll find out."

****

The Doctor placed his latest trophy in his hiding place and admired his work. Lined up on velvet boards and pinned into place, each scalp bore an identification label.

"When I hit fifty, I should celebrate my golden anniversary." He laughed at his own joke and stroked the clusters of long black hair, none as lustrous as they had once been. The stay-in hair conditioner helped keep the mementoes soft and pliable, but the natural shine was gone. He'd have to find another product soon. Maybe wig manufacturers had a technique to keep hair glossy.

"My number one. You fought like a cat. I liked that. It made it more fun when I watched you die." *More fun, but more dangerous.* He closed his eyes, reliving his first kill.

He had lived in Willimantic where the rent was cheap and had commuted to Farmington to medical school where the cost of living was high. Dissecting corpses that don't move or react or respond in any way was so unsatisfying. He had wanted someone— *something* that was terrified of him and his power and control. Each day on his drive to school, he'd seen a beauty, a flower in the broken concrete landscape of the old mill town. She'd looked so much like his mother it took his breath away. Over and over, he'd driven past the girl as she'd climbed into her ride. Then one day, he came across her on a back road, hitchhiking. Without even thinking, he seized the opportunity. He replayed the conversation in his head.

"Need a ride?"

"Thanks, yes." She flashed a dazzling smile. *"My driver called out sick."*

"Where do you work?" His mind ran through places to take her. He hadn't planned that part out. Where could he get her alone?

"At the casino. If you could get me to a bus stop, that would be good."

"Oh." He knew immediately what to do next. *"I'm in no rush. I can take you."*

The girl had been more athletic than expected. He'd been forced to drag her out of the car by her long black hair. All the while, he had chastised himself for his lack of preparation. *Would it have killed me to have duct tape and zip ties in the trunk? What kind of murderer am I? An unprepared one. Idiot.* Deep in the dark, buggy woods, he'd attempted to rape her, but hadn't been able to get an erection. *Her fault.* Enraged at his inability to make his cock leap to his command, he placed his hand over her mouth to shut her up.

She'd suffocated by accident. Furious at himself for bungling his first time, which should have been *epic,* he siphoned gas from his car and set her ablaze next to a stream. When her body had been charred to a crisp, he'd kicked her still smoking remains into the water. He remembered thinking there was no need to set the forest on fire and call attention to the body. It would take the cops months to find her. *After all, who could possibly be looking for this tramp?*

Much to his chagrin, not only was she someone's daughter, she was the daughter of the Mansfield Connecticut State Trooper's Sargent in charge of the barracks. Using dogs, the cops found her body, and the hunt was on for her killer. The Doctor realized he had to get rid of his car—or risk being discovered on traffic cameras—even in rural Eastern Connecticut. Selling his beater to a junk yard for parts, he bought another non-descript vehicle and decided to lay low until he could make a better plan.

Rape is stupid. I can have sex with anyone I want, male or female, without risk. They adore me and will do anything I ask, no matter how kinky. *I help them release their inner fantasies*. They want to wear corsets and use whips, be spread-eagled, tied to beds, and have candle wax dripped on them? Whatever they could imagine, he would deliver—with no problem getting it up, either. *I don't shit where I eat.* That would be stupid. Besides, none of his sexual conquests fit the bill for his murder lust. *The real fun is in the perfect kill.* Now he had the perfect, untraceable method. It was absolutely brilliant.

Before closing the large strong box, he opened his eyes and took one last tender look at his trophies. Shuddering with excitement, he fantasized about the women on his list in this target rich area. So many choices, so little time. *Who would be next?*

Chapter Nine

Hotel LaBelle ~*~ Billings, Montana

Sitting in his cruiser, Jacob rubbed his hands together and regretted leaving his gloves at home. His mother would read him the riot act, no doubt, but maybe not. She had other things on her mind—actually, another person on her mind.

After wrangling with Tommy Otterlegs, Uncle Dan, and tribal representatives, everyone had agreed that his mother's home—*his home*—was the best placement for Eddy—for now. Why? The Indian Child Welfare Law mandated finding a Native home for Eddy as soon as possible. His Jewish mother wasn't enrolled in the Crow Tribe, but by virtue of being a revered chief's widow, as well as the mother of the Tribal Chief of Police, who *was* a member of the tribe, the hurriedly convened committee had agreed she could serve as an emergency, but not a permanent placement. Eddy had been quite vocal in the meeting, yelling, "I have a right to say where I want to go, and I want to go with Auntie Esther. She'll keep me out of trouble." That part remained to be seen. Right now, the kid was sleeping in the spare bedroom, his stomach stuffed with roasted chicken, sweet potatoes, green beans, and challah smeared with globs of butter. Between gobbling food and chewing with his mouth open, the boy had talked non-stop. Maybe he belonged with Marjory Longjaw—now that woman was a talker.

Zena tapped at the window, and he unlocked the door. "Sorry it took me so long to change my clothes. Tallulah insisted on lending me some thermal underwear for my ride along."

"You'll thank her in the morning," he said with a grin. "Tonight's going to be below freezing."

She pulled her knit cap down, leaving a few wisps of red hair sticking out, making her look like a leprechaun heading off to the ski slopes. "Tell me again why you stay here?"

"This is Big Sky Country, and real Montanans can't bear to leave. And there are a lot of visitors who come to see the parks and decide to stay."

"Not sure I'm ready for that level of commitment," she grumbled. "I need to be wooed a bit more."

He placed his hand on her neck, and whispered, "Like this?"

The red-hot connection seared his lips—and his brain. This is the one, his animal side screamed at him. *Get her into bed. NOW!* The previously chilly space warmed up with the heady mix of sex pheromones.

Zena responded in kind, pulling his head closer, and running her fingers through his hair, sending frissons of pleasure down his scalp, back, and beyond.

The radio crackled, breaking the mood. "We have a possible break in at the Little Bear home."

Jacob pulled away, his lips still warm and tingling from the kiss. "Buzzkill." He grabbed the transmitter. "Isn't the house wrapped in crime tape?"

"No boss, after the ME's report of natural causes, we left it for the family to manage."

The family, which now consisted of a new father and a kid, was most likely too occupied to keep an eye on the property. That meant the house was open to robbers and druggies, often one and the same.

"On my way." He clicked the transmitter off and turned to Zena. "Wooing to be continued."

"Just as well." She adjusted her jacket and scarf. "The damn stick shift was getting in the way."

Chuckling, he put the car in gear. "I like the way you think."

"And way too many layers to deal with," she complained. "If we could do this in our fur, it would be much simpler."

"That," he choked between gales of laughter, "would be quite a sight. I can see it now. You and I shift right after we roll up to the house, so all the neighbors and rubberneckers see is two wolves, in the squad car, one driving and one riding shotgun."

"I didn't mean to make it a circus," she objected. "Are you going to tell me you don't use your other abilities to clear cases?"

"I do." He smiled. "But there's a time and place for those skills. Though I've been known to conduct some midnight tracking for missing people and fugitives."

"Then why wouldn't we do it here? Don't you want to see that house with your other senses? We already know there's a serial killer out there. With the ME's instant decision of death by natural causes, I'm betting the CSI team wasn't all that attentive to clues beyond checking her medicine cabinet for heart pills."

Pulling in front of the Little Bear house, he put the car in park, and cocked his head at Zena. "You want to get naked with me?"

She grinned. "Now?"

He nodded. "Once we're inside, we can drop the shades and do what we need to do. You in?"

By way of answer, she leaped out of the car. "What are you waiting for?"

A couple of teenagers loitered around the house, smoking. They raised their chins at Jacob as he approached, and the distinctive odor of pot enveloped him. "Joe, Tommy. Sup, guys? You see anything?"

Joe shrugged. "Nah, I didn't see nothing."

"So, who called?"

Tommy, the taller of the two boys, inclined his head toward the house next door. "Grandma Grady. She's the neighborhood watch commander."

The other boy snickered. "She'll call in for us being out after midnight. Says we can't be up to any good."

He doubted these kids were working on a community service project in the middle of the night. "Well, are you?"

"Hey, man, we like to get some fresh air at night, look at the stars, have a smoke. There's no curfew is there?"

"Not at this time." The last curfew had been imposed due to three meth related murders. These guys wouldn't be any help. "You guys have a nice evening."

"Thanks, Officer Friendly," Tommy sneered.

As they walked toward the neighbor's home, Zena asked in a low voice, "What happened to respect for elders?"

"You'll still see it, but those two? They're working on getting rich. It's only a matter of time before they go from smoking marijuana to cooking meth."

"You don't go after pot smoking? Isn't it illegal in this state?"

Jacob shook his head. "Legal for medicinal use, not for recreational use. As short-handed as we are, we can't afford to do the paperwork. By the time we'd get to court, the kids would have a prescription from a shady doctor. You have to pick your battles."

A round-faced woman with gray hair pulled back in a bun opened the door as Jacob raised his fist to knock. "About time you got here."

"Yes, ma'am. I was on the other side of the rez. I understand you were the caller. Can you tell me what you saw?"

Mrs. Grady eyed Zena with suspicion and crossed her arms over her ample chest. "Who's the woman with you? Never seen her before."

"This is FBI Special Agent Zena Adalwolf. She's assisting us with an investigation."

Zena raised a hand in greeting but remained silent.

"About an hour ago, when I called 9-1-1, I noticed some lights on in the Little Bear house." Mrs. Grady paused and took a breath. "The power is off there, guess the family forgot to pay the electric bill. Their pipes are going to freeze. Someone should let them know."

"Yes, ma'am, I'll be sure to do that. Tell me about the lights."

"Had to be flashlights, bobbing up and down, like they were looking for something. You better check to see if the appliances are still in there. Stoves are valuable. I know I could use a new one."

"Yes, ma'am. We will do that. Anything else? Did you see anyone exit the building?" He didn't want to walk into a trap. It wouldn't be the first time some thugs were waiting for him on the other side of the door of an unoccupied house.

"Why yes I did." She nodded vigorously.

Repressing a sigh, Jacob said, "Can you tell me how many people you saw? Which direction did they go?"

"Two. And they're standing right over there, smoking pot."

He tipped his hat. "Thank you, ma'am. You have a good night."

The teens howled with laughter as they approached them. "Mystery solved, Officer Friendly?"

"I don't know, boys. Mrs. Grady claims you were in the Little Bear house. Is that correct?"

The boys shook their heads.

"We been right here for the past three hours, enjoying the fine weather." Tommy said.

"Then we won't find your fingerprints in the house?" Jacob pressed.

The jeering bravado plummeted off their faces. "You wouldn't actually do that, would you?"

"I like to clear my cases, so yes, I would. Unless you have some insights to offer?"

"The door was open," Joe blurted. "We were worried someone might rob them."

"Oh, so you were being good neighbors, checking on the place," he said. "Is that right?"

"Yeah, yeah," Tommy chimed in. "Good neighbors, like that insurance company."

"I'm guessing you used the flashlight on your smart phone to poke around?"

Joe gulped. "Yeah."

"Find anything good?" Jacob pulled a notepad out

of his pocket. He was enjoying watching the boys sweat. Maybe he *could* put the fear of God into these criminal wannabes.

"No." Tommy jumped in. "The place was stripped, man. No furniture, no clothes, no appliances, completely empty. It was like a creepy haunted house. We didn't stay long."

Maybe Tommy had taken care of the property. He'd need to call him in the morning to tell him to put a better lock on the place before it was vandalized or used as a drug house.

"Boys, I'm not going to arrest you." He knew damn well without a criminal complaint in writing from the owner it would be tough going. "But I am going to give you a citation for loitering. Your parents will be notified, and this will be on your permanent record."

"Permanent record?" Joe retorted. "What is this, Catholic School?"

"Yeah," Jacob answered. "But without the nuns. Now go home."

As the teens sauntered away, Zena said, "Well, that was fun."

"Nine times out of ten, the calls for service are routine." He shook his head.

"It's the tenth call that gets you."

Zena whispered, "You still interested in getting naked with me?"

****

Inside, the house was almost as cold as the outside. Silver plumes puffing with each breath, Zena surveyed the kitchen with her Maglite. The kids weren't wrong. The place was stripped to the wood flooring. Stepping over to the sink, she turned the faucet on. No water came out. "Looks like someone has already winterized the place."

"Must have been Tommy's wife, Wanda. She was super organized *before* it was fashionable."

"Hooray, Wanda," Zena said. "What do you think?"

Jacob drew close to her and pulled her into an embrace. "I think it would be a good idea to scope the place out of uniform."

His kiss landed with precision and heat, thrilling her from head to toe. This guy knew how to warm a woman up. She killed the light, pulled his head down, and ran her fingers through his hair, knocking his hat off. Then she unzipped his jacket and tugged it off his broad shoulders.

As she undressed him, his hands roamed over her, removing her hat, jacket, and turtleneck. When he arrived at the thermal underwear, he laughed. "Thanks, Tallulah."

Now she was pulling at his pants, unbuckling the belt, groping with the zipper. An impressive erection sprang to attention under her stiff with cold, fumbling fingers.

He groaned. "Woman, empty house or not, if you keep doing that, there's going to be a problem."

She laughed. "Big trouble?"

"Yes." He pried her hands away from his groin. "I'm on duty, you're on duty. We should probably save this for another time."

Zena mock pouted. "Okay."

"I'll go to another room, give you a little privacy."

"Thanks." Thoughtful *and* a good kisser. She looked forward to the opportunity to test his other romantic skills. Placing her clothes in a neat pile on the kitchen counter, she shivered in the cold and called her inner beast.

Her arms and legs grew shorter, her face lengthened, and her ears became pointed. A red aura surrounded her, shimmering as her thick red and gray fur erupted, giving her the perfect coat for any weather. The ruddy glow faded as the transformation came to an end. Falling onto all fours, she began to sniff the air.

A massive gray wolf, fur tipped with silver, entered the room, thrilling and arousing her. He was as handsome in this form as in his human form.

"Why thank you," he chuffed.

"You can hear me?" She'd better guard her mind better. *"I thought werewolves could only communicate if they were in the same clan."*

A mental laugh. *"That and if they are destined to be mates."*

"D'oh." If she could have blushed, she would have. Better get back to work. *"See or smell anything?"*

He shook his head. *"Bathroom was squeaky clean, literally. Bleach residue. Vinegar odor in the bedrooms, probably from mopping the floor. Want to do the kitchen together?"*

She nodded. *"You're taller than me, so why don't you take the cabinets?"*

He stood on his hind legs and began pushing the doors open with his muzzle.

Nose to the floor, Zena began in one corner, going down each crack in the floorboards with care. Halfway through, she stopped and lifted her head. *"Over here!"*

Jacob dropped to all fours and padded over to her.

"What is it?"

"There's something wedged in there." Carefully sliding a claw into the thin space, she hooked something white and pulled it out. *"Well, that's interesting."*

Nostrils flaring, Zena lay on the floor with her paws out, transfixed by a torn packet of headache powder.

Chapter Ten

Organic Grocers ~*~ Billings, Montana

Carrying a small plastic basket, the Doctor
Doctor entered the grocery store under the watchful
gaze of the founder, a smiling woman in the center of a
mural of a humongous flower. The portrait's eyes
seemed to follow him as he inspected the shelves of
homeopathic remedies, crystals, CBD oil, massage, and
yoga supplies at the front of the store. He paused at an
endcap featuring a large display of winter wellness
products. *Boost Your Immune System with Elderberry
Tea!*

A pimple-faced teen with, long black hair pulled
back into a ponytail, approached him. He was an
Indian, that was certain, and he had nice shiny hair—
but he was the wrong gender.

"Are you looking for something in particular, sir?"

The Doctor glanced at the kid's name tag and
flashed a winning smile, the one that charmed men,
women, and children. "Hi, Jimmy. This is my first time
here, so I'm looking around."

"Let me know if you need anything." The eager
employee turned and approached another customer,
repeating his question.

The Doctor wondered how the kid would respond
if he'd said, "Why yes, I'm in the market for someone

to kill. I need a beautiful Indian woman with long black hair who looks like the mother who abandoned me when I was nine and left me to rot in foster homes. Do you have any of those in stock?" Jimmy didn't seem like he would be prepared to answer *that* kind of request.

Smiling at his own joke, he kept looking around. Pedophiles lurked around school yards. He liked grocery stores for the same reason—a target rich environment. This place with its hippie vibe would be his happy hunting ground. Part of him enjoyed the thrill of the chase, the anticipation of the kill. The longer it took him to find the right woman, the more exciting it was when he took her life. He hated the easy prey. That old lady in the hospital? Like shooting ducks in a barrel. A total letdown, especially when they closed the damn door for the code, and he couldn't watch from his hiding place across the hall.

Esther. She was the problem. That frigging midwife haunted him, showing up at the wrong place at the wrong time. What the hell was she doing in the hospital right then with that skinny little boy? If the Doctor didn't have a firm *don't shit where you eat* rule, that woman would be right up there on the top of his list, and he'd enjoy every second of choking the life out of her. *Bitch.*

Glancing down the corridors lined with products, he decided to hit the sides of the store where critical food, like eggs, milk, meat, and bread would be. Women usually clustered in those sections, looking for the sell by date and day-old items. The dairy aisle offered an assortment of women, mostly white, their pale skin matching the milk. Deciding it might look odd if he didn't purchase anything, he placed a carton of half and half in his basket and headed to the cleaning aisle. The housewives had to replace their supplies *sometime*.

A lone teenager restocking the shelves looked up and smiled. "May I help you, sir?"

"No, thanks." The Doctor tamped down a desire to snap the boy's head off. *Where are the Indian women?*

He stomped to the produce section—and froze. His heart giddy-upped in his chest, skipping a few beats along the way. A raven-haired amazon in a plaid flannel shirt, a down vest, jeans, and metal tipped cowboy boots examined a pile of pumpkins. Long strands of lustrous hair draped her face as she bent down to pick up the most symmetrical one. Her vest opened as she stood, revealing a dog tag necklace. *Hers? Or her boyfriend's?* Either way, her confident air and military bearing drew him in. He could not take his gaze off her.

She turned and faced him. "You looking for something?"

If only this beauty knew what he wanted, she wouldn't stand there with a furrowed brow—staring at him like she would sooner shoot him than talk to him.

"Sorry." Cotton-mouthed, he practically choked on his words. "I couldn't help but notice you selected the prettiest one in the pile. Do you think you could pick one for me? I'm terrible at this stuff, and I'm supposed to bring something festive to the office holiday party."

She glanced at his basket. "Hope you aren't planning to get a lot."

He gave a self-deprecating laugh. "I'm new, wanted to check the place out, and get a gourd or whatever."

Quirking an eyebrow, the woman curved over again, affording him a glance of her fine ass. When she handed him a perfect orange globe, the diamond ring on her hand glittered. His stomach fluttered. *Married.* He couldn't wait to run his fingers through her hair, feel the silky tresses, inhale the perfume of shampoo—and watch her die in his arms.

"Thanks." He turned his thousand-watt grin on her. "What is your name?"

She frowned. "None of your business."

He nodded, gave her a stiff bow, and backed away. *Rude. She will be so much fun to kill.*

For the next thirty minutes, he stalked the woman, slinking behind stacks of natural sodas, tall displays of cookies, and pallets of bread. At last, she headed for the check-out stand. Throwing subtlety out the window, he stepped in line behind her.

The beauty gave him an annoyed look and placed her items on the belt, including several boxes of lidocaine patches.

"Miss?" he said with grave respect.

She locked gazes with him. Had he been superstitious, he would have said she could see through to his soul. "Yes?"

"Is someone hurt? I know how to treat pain."

The woman turned to the clerk. "I'll help you bag." She moved to the end of the cashier's counter and began opening her reusable totes.

He couldn't let her get away. "I'm a Doctor. I can help you with the pain."

The woman didn't respond and placed items into the bag at a faster pace.

"Is it for arthritis? I bet you're Native American. I

have natural remedies for pain."

Ignoring him, she pulled out her wallet and retrieved some cash. He tried to get a glimpse of her driver's license, but she pocketed it too fast.

He continued, speaking as if to a child or a person for whom English is a second language. "I can use natural healing herbs to help you with any pain you may be having. I'm a Doctor at the Crow Indian Health Service. I'm extremely familiar with natural remedies."

The clerk handed the woman her receipt. "Thanks, Emma. Say hi to your hubby for me."

Emma. Such an old-fashioned name. Four simple letters, but so important to him.

She looked him squarely in the eye. "Doctor?"

He had her attention at last. Turn on the charisma, smile, reel her in. "Yes?"

"The only pain I have at this moment is *you*. I suggest you peddle your potions elsewhere. Some women may think you're charming—but not this one. If you ever bother me again, you will regret it."

His face heated, and the happy gallop in his chest slowed to a dull thudding. *Fucking bitch. I will find you and enjoy every moment of your death.*

The cashier's perky voice interrupted his fantasies. "Did you find everything you needed?"

"What? Oh, yes, I did." He tapped his toe, impatient to get out to the parking lot to find that woman.

"You know," she chirped, "I couldn't help but overhear you talking to Emma. I have a bad back from standing on my feet all day. Do you think your natural pain relievers would work for me?"

The Doctor took a closer look at the clerk who'd

been nothing but background noise before. Long, black hair, high cheekbones, and definitely Indian. All attributes on the plus side, and she wasn't wearing a wedding ring. A bit plumper than he liked, but...

"My dear," he said in low-voice and a tone reserved for lovers, "I have a remedy that will get rid of your back pain *permanently*."

****

Hotel LaBelle ~*~ Billings, Montana

Zena woke up and stretched, every muscle in her body aching from the night before. A good feeling. She loved being in her wolf form and reveled in the morning after soreness and hunger. Shape-shifting required a lot of energy, and like an athlete feeling the burn, the pain reaffirmed her ability to transform into her animal side. She had the best of both worlds. Well, almost. If Jacob had woken up next to her, then all would be perfect. But the man was a pillar of propriety, insisting on waiting until they were off the clock to move forward in their relationship. *Damn.* First, she'd been besieged with guys who only want to hump her, then she connects with one who acts like sex is a sacrament. Lolling in bed, drawing out the pleasure of the soft mattress and pillows, she finally sat up and realized she was not alone.

An elderly Native American woman with long braids, wearing a buckskin dress covered in elk teeth, stood at the foot of her bed. Smiling, she raised a hand in greeting—and disappeared. Simply shimmered out of sight. The only sign of her having been there at all was a feather that drifted to the floor in a slow, lazy swirl.

Zena snapped her mouth shut, swallowed, and surveyed the room. Throwing the blankets back, she leaped out of bed and strode to the place where the woman had stood. A large black and white feather rested on the area rug. She picked it up, examining it from every angle.

Eagle, no doubt about it.

After placing the quill with care on her nightstand, she leaped into the shower, brushed her teeth, ran her fingers through her hair, and jump-hopped into her pants before grabbing the rest of her clothes. Dressed at last, she snatched up the feather, stuck it behind her ear, and headed downstairs.

The smell of coffee and bacon called to her. Stomach rumbling, she strode into the kitchen, happy to see both Lucius and Tallulah. "Good morning!"

"You sleep well?" Tallulah inquired. "It can be tough trying to snooze in a strange place."

"Like a baby, except I didn't cry. Do you sell the mattresses?" Zena asked. "I think you could have a sideline business with them, like the hotels in Vegas."

Lucius guffawed. "Now that girl has a head for business." He placed a platter of scrambled eggs and bacon on the table, along with a basket of biscuits. "Salt, pepper, butter, and jam are next to you. Coffee?"

"Yes, please, a large cappuccino with lots of caffeine." She began piling food on her plate—and stopped. "Sorry, I'm being rude. I'm starving."

"Eat," Tallulah said. "Where'd you get that feather?"

"From a little old Indian lady who showed up in my room and then disappeared," Zena said between bites. "She dropped it on the floor when she went poof."

"Beautiful," Tallulah and Lucius said at the same

time.

"You mentioned her the other day, said she'd pop in and out. I didn't realize you meant that literally."

Tallulah glanced at her husband. "She must like you."

"Yup, that there is a special gift for you. The Crow give those to honor people." He cocked his head. "She's a funny one. Gets around, knows more than most. She must've figured out you're helping the tribe."

"How was your ride along?" Tallulah asked.

"Great. Met a bunch of interesting characters. Thank you for that underwear. Most helpful in my human form."

Tallulah raised her eyebrows. "Oh?"

Zena could feel the heat racing to her face. "Jacob and I had a coming out party last night during an investigation. Did you know that when he's in his wolf form, his coat shimmers like it's dipped in silver? So pretty. And he's big, larger than any other wolf shifter I've ever seen. And I grew up in a big pack in West Virginia. Not one of those guys can hold a candle to him." She sighed. "So much fun."

"Darlin', there is something in the water. Every time we get a guest, we wind up with a wedding. Do you think we can bottle and sell it as Love Potion Number Ten?"

Tallulah laughed. "You are a relentless matchmaker."

"Okay, you got me." Zena's face burned even more. "I'm smitten. But who wouldn't be?"

"The criminals, that's who," Lucius answered. "Jacob is a very effective tribal police officer. Crooks hate to see him coming."

Tallulah nodded. "Too bad he has that blind spot when it comes to his uncle."

"Redhawk?" Zena sat up straighter. "Why? What did he do?"

Lucius shook his head. "We shouldn't spread rumors."

"Gossip?" Zena parried. "You mean important intelligence that might have some element of truth at its base?"

"Well, when you put it that way. You didn't hear none of this from us."

She nodded.

"Rumor has it, he might have had his hand in the till when his brother, Joseph, was chief. Daniel was the treasurer, in charge of making sure the enrollment checks were distributed to members of the tribe…" He paused. "Story goes, Joseph—Jacob's father—confronted Daniel in front of the council, called him a thief."

"What happened?" Zena's question slid out on an exhalation. "How did Daniel get to be in charge of the tribal council?"

"Jacob's father was murdered. The case was never solved, no charges for embezzlement, and Daniel was elected chairman."

"That certainly sounds fishy, but I'm not sure that makes him a criminal," Zena mused. "Jacob told me he was there when his father was killed. Still can't recall that night."

"Some things are better forgotten," Tallulah said. "I'm grateful Miriam can't recall her ordeal of being kidnapped."

Lucius squeezed his wife's hand. "She's a happy

little girl. Thank God."

Zena fell silent. Was Jacob happy? Or was he still searching for the memory of that night and his father's killer? Some said family members needed truth for closure, but that was only partially true. She knew who murdered her sisters and that he'd been brought down. She also knew who shot and killed her mother. But, in both instances, the truth had not set her free.

Chapter Eleven

Crow Indian Health Service ~~ Crow Agency,
Montana*

The Doctor sat alone in the clinic break room and
tore open the hand-written envelope without a return
address. A yellowed newspaper clipping fluttered to the
floor, and he stooped down to pick it up, glancing at the
headline that screamed *Local Girl Murdered*. Neck
prickling with unease, he scanned the article. As he did,
he relived that day in the woods seven years ago. His
heart fluttered with excitement. *I was thinking about
you, Number One*. They got details right but missed the
most important one—*the identity of the killer*. In a way
he was grateful to her. She'd been his teacher. He
learned from that first kill that he had to plan and
prepare better. Each subsequent victim had added to his
edification. Now, he was smarter than ever. He'd
become more prepared and proficient—the kind of man
mothers should warn their daughters about

*Almost fifty—count them—fifty kills. Eat your heart
out, Casanova Killer, twenty victims is nothing. Watch
out, Dr. Death, I'm catching up to you. I'm going to
beat your record of two-hundred patients.* Chuckling,
he folded the article, set it aside, and began to decipher
the spidery handwriting.

Dear Son.

He clenched his teeth. Him again.

I'm know it's hard for you to believe that I'm your pappy. What you see now is an old alcoholic, in and out of jail, now out for good because I'm dying. I need to tell you some things before I die. I grew up in Georgia and moved to Connecticut to work in the textile factories in Willimantic. I met your mama, Rose Robin, at the factory. She was tall and slender, with long black hair, from the Indian side of her family. She was working the line and we fell in love. The factory closed, we were both out of work, and your mama got pregnant—with you. When the casino opened, it saved our little family from starving. Your mama sold Bingo cards. She was so good, they kept promoting her. I stayed home and took care of you. But I didn't like it. Hated that my wife was supporting the family, not me. The bottle became my friend—and then baby number two was on the way.

The Doctor paused, looking up. The other child in the old photo?

Your mama gave us a beautiful little girl. But she knew she couldn't support two kids and a lousy drunk. I agreed to put our baby girl up for adoption to give her a better life. The couple who took your sister had a still birth. Rose said they cried when they took your sister. They were a loving family. And he was a police officer, not a broken-down alcoholic with a string of broken promises and jailtime. Your mama died when I was in for a long stretch. You became a ward of the state—and I lost you and your sister, Violet.

From somewhere deep within, something—a muscle memory of what might have been grief and regret once upon a time—plucked at the Doctor like a child pulling at his mother's skirt. *No*. It couldn't be.

She was murdered. Her body was found in the woods in Eastern Connecticut, burned beyond recognition. They identified Violet through her dental records.

The beauty. The girl he'd picked up hitchhiking. Rage simmered as tears blurred the last words.

If you want to talk, I'm at the Cowboy Motel, room three.

The Doctor closed his eyes and sank back in the chair. *His sister.* The absurdity of it all—the old man shows up eight years after that damn DNA test, seven years after his first kill, only to tell him—without realizing it—that he had killed his one and only sister? Bowing his head, he covered his face with his hands—and began to laugh. He pulled his tear-soaked hands away and realized he'd been sobbing like a little girl.

What kind of man allows his wife to put his child up for adoption? This was all that old fool's fault. What kind of twisted logic allowed this stupid sonovabitch to think he could show up and make amends for ruining his life? If this piece of shit had simply stopped drinking, he would have never been put in that series of hell holes where he'd been beaten, burned, and sexually molested for years—his life would have been so different, better. But no, this selfish burned out walking dead man had decided it was all about him, and his family didn't matter. Now this human dung-beetle decided to act as if he gave a shit?

Folding the letter and article and tucking both back into the envelope, the Doctor wiped his face. A little while to quitting time. Invitation in hand, he would go to the man reeking of death soon—and help him with his pain.

****

Esther waved at the administrator deep in conversation with Dr. Turner at the receptionist's desk. The clinic manager kept shaking her head no, and the Doctor tapped the counter with his index finger repeatedly. *Ugh.* She wondered what new demand the pain in the butt physician was making on their already strained budget. The last thing he'd requested was a private office, claiming he couldn't *possibly* preserve patient confidentiality in a shared office. He acted as if the rest of the staff didn't know privacy laws and only he, God's gift to medicine, knew the one true way to run things.

Quitting time, hallelujah. It had been one of those days when she'd barely had time to empty her bladder, much less eat. She entered the break room and spotted Dr. Bob at a corner table. Head bowed, a white envelope in his hand, he didn't look up when she came in.

"Sorry to bother you. I need to get into the fridge to retrieve the lunch I never had time to eat."

Startled, he looked up with an expression of confusion. "Oh, sure, sorry." Stuffing the packet into his pocket, he stood so fast he knocked the chair into the wall. "Let me get out of your way."

"Are you okay, Bob? You look upset." She'd never seen him look like this before. If she had to guess, she'd say he was grief stricken.

"I'm fine," he said curtly. "I have some personal business to attend to. Nothing I can't handle."

"Okay." She plucked her lunch bag out of the overfilled fridge. "We need to clean this thing out before the holiday party." She glanced over her shoulder. "What did you sign up to bring?"

"Fresh pumpkin with cinnamon and brown sugar, but who cares? Nobody truly wants to come. I hate office parties. We're forced to attend, make small talk with people who wouldn't say hello to us outside of this place, and pretend we're happy."

Slack-jawed, Esther stared at him. Where was the Teddy Bear, the guy all the adolescents adored? "Something happen, Bob? I'm here if you want to talk about anything."

"As if you'd give a crap." Turning on his heel, Bob shot his parting words at her over his shoulder. "Maybe the world would be better off without some people."

Was he having a bad day? Or was it a suicide announcement? She shuddered, and her unfed stomach roiled with dread. Or could it have been a threat? She had no choice but to inform the clinic administrator. Violence in healthcare settings was a taboo topic. No one ever wanted to talk about the elephant in the room. She wondered how many lives had been lost because people refused to get involved. This pachyderm was getting some attention STAT. Hoping to catch up with the doctor to make sense of the conversation, perhaps stop him from self-harm, she sped after Bob. She searched the exam rooms, the shared office space, and the utility rooms, earning puzzled glances from the few workers left in the place. She ran to the security guard. "Have you seen Dr. Bob?"

The big guy in the gray uniform pointed at the door. "You just missed him."

****

FBI Office ~*~ Billings, Montana

The moment Zena and Jacob walked into the borrowed office space the evening after they searched the Littlebear house in wolf form, his phone began to ring. Zena pulled out a rolling chair and logged into VICAP, the violent criminal apprehension program. She began searching for serial killers who preyed on Native American women.

"Mom, you can't put an APB out on someone because they've had a bad day." Jacob shook his head and rolled his eyes at Zena. "I understand your concern. This is not a police matter. I get how you feel. Your psychic senses may have been tingling, but that is not going to count in a court of law if we make a false arrest."

His mother's tone rose, and Zena heard the panic in her voice, if not the exact words.

"What if I use some other, shall we say, channels to take a look?" He paused. "Tallulah or Bronco. I'm sure one of them would be happy to help. Does that work?" A pause. "Good. I'll make the call. Hang tight and keep Eddy out of trouble."

He pressed the end button. "My mother."

"I gathered. Trouble?"

"Yeah," he nodded. "Kind of. One of my mother's co-workers is acting strange. She's worried he's going to hurt someone, maybe himself or other people."

"Somebody needs to do a threat assessment." Violence in the workplace was a real thing, nothing to laugh at. "Did she tell her boss?"

"Yes, and yes. The guy has no record—had to have a criminal background check before coming to Indian Health Services. Teenagers like him. He gets their angst. He and his spouse were supposed to be assigned in Billings together. But that didn't happen. He's been fighting with the bureaucracy ever since he landed here. She says something triggered him today."

"Who is Bronco?"

"My cousin Emma's husband. He's a remote viewer, like Tallulah."

"You guys are very casual with all this classified information." She lowered her voice even though the door of her borrowed workspace was closed, and the rest of the agents were gone for the day. "Most people would be a bit more cautious about sharing with outsiders."

He stepped closer and pulled her into a hug. "You're not an outsider anymore. Not after last night."

The heat in the office rose ten degrees and matched the flames burning her cheeks. "Keep your voice down."

He shrugged. "We worked a case together. What's wrong with that?"

"You make it sound like we did something—" She looked up at his eyes, now that quicksilver color, the color of his wolf. "Stop laughing at me."

"We got naked together," he whispered, and bumped her groin with his.

A wave of desire raced from her core to her breasts and she gasped. "Stop—" The room filled with a dizzying mix of his and her desire, ramping up her lust.

He nuzzled her neck and shoved her against the desk, pushing between her legs. The throbbing intensified to an unbearable burn, and her hips rose involuntarily. "I'm. At. Work," she gasped.

Grabbing her buttocks, he pulled her close to him, ground his hardness into her heated center, and whispered, "Exciting, isn't it?"

She threw her head back, suppressing a moan. Nuzzling the vee of her blouse, he nipped and licked at the base of her neck, sending shudders of pleasure down her spine.

"That feel good?"

She suppressed a moan and husked, "Yes, oh yes."

"We're off duty," he murmured against her lips. "Time to take it to the next level, don't you think?"

"Oh, y—"

Her phone howled, and he jumped back. "Is that you?"

"Yes." She fumbled in her pocket and looked at the caller ID. "It's a text from the crime lab." Tapping at the screen, Zena enlarged the file for a better look. "It's the results of the tox screen from the bottled water we found in the park—and the packet we found at Eddy's house." She turned the phone and slid through the documents. "They're the same. Strychnine—like we guessed—but there's something else." She squinted at the comments on the end of the report. "What the hell is brucine?"

He pulled his phone out and ran a quick search. "An alkaloid. Odorless, bitter flavor, less toxic than strychnine, but if you consume two milligrams, it has the same effect as strychnine. As in you convulse and die. Often found in traditional medicines used to treat inflammation and pain."

All traces of lust dissipated, and their gazes locked.

Flipping through her texts, she said, "I know Tommy demanded an ME report on his mother."

"On it." Jacob put his phone on speaker. "Joe, where are the results on Mrs. Otterlegs?"

"Well, hello to you, too," the ME said, his voice laced with sarcasm. "I'm fine, thanks for asking."

"Thank you for rushing the autopsy and the tox screen," Zena said, attempting to soothe his wounded feelings. "I know you've been working day and night on this."

Jacob rolled his eyes and shook his head.

"Why thank you. It's nice *someone* appreciates all I the work I do."

"What's your price? Donuts, coffee, wine?" Jacob asked.

"Twenty-five-year-old single malt scotch and a carton of cigarettes," the ME said and blew out a long breath. "This one made me take up smoking again. Filthy habit."

Zena jumped in. "What'd you find?"

"In addition to her heart meds and all the other stuff they pumped into her for the code, the poor lady had enough brucine in her system to kill a moose. Not to mention a good-sized chunk of scalp taken out of the back of her head. Mattress stitches, the *worst* suturing I've ever seen—and I'm a freaking pathologist. Our patients never complain about their scars."

"Thanks, Joe," Zena said. "I won't buy you cancer sticks, but I promise the whiskey will be on your desk tomorrow."

"I needed to quit anyway."

Jacob ended the call. "Too bad we don't have any evidence from the first victim back from the start of summer. I'd bet my mother's pot roast she was his first victim."

"First victim here in Billings, maybe, but not his first kill." Zena shook her head. She pointed to the timeline on the whiteboard in her office. "He killed Kimani Fleetfoot in mid-June. Then, approximately six weeks later in mid-July, he killed Eddy's mother, Coral Little Bear. He took a break—maybe he went out of town, or was in jail? Nothing for two months, then he killed your friend, Skye Martinez, in mid-October. Here it is the third week in November, and he kills Mrs. Otterlegs. Why is the middle of the month important to him? Something triggers him. An anniversary? But of what?"

Jacob tapped Mrs. Otterlegs' name. "She's not his type. Mrs. Otterlegs was twice the age of the other victims."

"He does have a preferred profile," she agreed. "Native, female, mid-thirties. Didn't she have unusually dark hair for a grandmother?"

"Yeah. She didn't go gray. Sort of like my mother. And it was long."

"Maybe she was convenient, a substitute for what or who he actually wants?"

Jacob rubbed his chin. "He gets triggered, something or someone blocks him from his usual prey. And she's a sitting duck there in the hospital."

"Eddy said she told him a doctor came in and took a biopsy. And your mother said Mrs. Otterlegs told them she had a headache, poured some powder into her water, and sipped it." Zena put her hands on her hips. "Had to be the same powder we found at Coral Little Bear's house. Did she bring it in from home or did the doctor give her the poison?"

"Anyone in scrubs can pass for a physician," Jacob countered. "Like in the mystery, *The Invisible Man*, no one ever suspected the postman because he was always in the background."

"That headache packet we found contained brucine, as did the bottle of water we found near Skye," Zena mused out loud. "Too bad the hospital disposed of everything in the room after Mrs. Otterlegs coded. Would have been nice to have that packet to definitively connect the dots."

"Chairman Dan may have been onto something. Maybe the killer does take pieces of scalp as trophies."

"Yech." Zena stuck her tongue out in disgust. "What's he doing, making a wig for himself?"

"Anything's possible."

"In addition to his type, there's one more common denominator we need to pursue."

He cocked his head. "Go on."

"Who do you trust and where do you go when you're an Indian woman and you need advice about managing pain?"

"You're more than a pretty face, you're brilliant!" Jacob grabbed Zena and pulled her in for a lip searing kiss. "It's time for you to really meet my mother."

Chapter Twelve

Crow Reservation ~*~ Billings, Montana

Esther pulled her SUV into the driveway and turned to Eddy. "Thanks for going to the grocery store with me. Think you can help me unload the trunk?"

"Sure." He grinned. "What's for dinner?"

"The bison burgers you picked out." She popped the back door. "And butternut squash and some of those green things you made faces at in the produce aisle."

"I hate broccoli." He scrunched up his face. "It smells like farts."

"That's why you eat it the day you buy it." She laughed and lifted two heavy reusable bags. "You know what smells like farts when it's cooking?"

He shook his head.

"Dried lima beans." She grimaced. "I can't stand them. My mother made me eat them once a week in a soup on Friday."

"Why would she do that to you?" The bag with the eggs slipped in his hands, and Esther grabbed it before it hit the ground.

"A couple of reasons. She was a Holocaust survivor, a child in a displaced persons camp. Food was hard to come by, so they ate a lot of beans. Plus, she was religious. She kept the Sabbath. No working. Bean soup can be left on a low burner all day so you don't have to light a fire."

He shook his head. "I thought Indians had some weird traditions."

"Different." She laughed. "Not strange."

An owl hooted in the distance, and Eddy looked around. "I don't see him."

"Tiger is very good at hiding—unless you threaten him."

"Got that right," Eddy said. "My arm's all healed up, not even a scar."

"Glad to hear it." She smiled to herself. *I still have the touch. Like my mother.* "Hold on, let me get the door."

A horn honked.

Ugh. The last person I want to see today.

Daniel jumped out of his pick-up truck and ran to her door. "Let me take those for you. You shouldn't be doing all that heavy lifting."

"Thanks. I've got them."

He wrestled her for the bags. She hung onto the handles for as long as she dared, but fearing they'd tear, she let go. Now she'd have to let him in the house. *Dammit.* She turned the key and opened the door.

Out of nowhere, the resident great horned owl dove at the man with an earsplitting shriek. Ducking his head and hunching his shoulders, Daniel lunged into the house as if a cougar was on his tail.

Jessie growled and struggled to her feet. Esther suppressed a giggle. *Tiger and Jessie don't like you.* She petted Jessie. "It's okay, girl."

"So, Eddy," Daniel said, rubbing his hands, "how's Auntie Esther treating you?"

"Great." The boy placed the totes on the kitchen

table, crossed his arms over his chest, and raised his chin. "Why are you here?"

The kid's a mind reader.

"Son, I want to be sure you have everything you need. It's my job to look after the tribe."

The boy opened his mouth to retort something like *You're not my dad!* no doubt, but Esther silenced him with a look. "Eddy, why don't you go do your homework? I'll start dinner. Then we can find a new comic book for you to read after we eat."

A quick study, the boy nodded, frowned at Daniel, and left the room.

"He's a good kid," Esther said with a smile. "Truly helpful."

Daniel snorted. "Sure, whatever you say."

Wishing for the thousandth time that he would leave, she put the groceries away.

"Actually, I was hoping your son would be home. I need to talk to him."

"He's working a case right now, as you know. Not sure when he'll get here. Don't you have his phone number?" *Please, please, please go away.*

"This can't be discussed on the phone." He glanced at his watch. "I'm in no rush. I'll take a cup of coffee, as long as it's no bother."

As if you care.

"Of course not," she said through gritted teeth. "Cream and two sugars?"

"You remembered. I'm touched."

Mentally kicking herself for even appearing to give a rat's ass about him, she motioned him to a chair and grabbed a mug out of the cupboard.

"That dinner offer still stands. If you don't want to

go to the Billings Club, we could find some other place."

Facing away from him, she closed the lid to the coffee maker a little too hard. *The man did not take no for answer.* The smarmy smile, his fake concern, his over the top heartiness. He made her skin crawl. She wanted to scream at him to get out of her house. Out of respect for the fact that he was her dead husband's brother and Jacob's uncle, she tolerated his presence in her life. But she would never accept him in her bed. *Never.*

Headlights shone through the living room windows.

"Maybe that's Jacob now," Esther said with a bit too much enthusiasm. "You can have your chat and get on with the rest of your evening."

The front door opened. She wanted to cheer.

"Hi, Mom," her son said with a shy grin. His eyes sparkled like his father's when he looked at her on their wedding day. "I've brought someone who wants to talk to you."

A striking redhead stepped in the door and smiled. Surrounded by a rosy glow, she reminded Esther of a pixie with her flaming locks.

"She was at the hospital with me the other day, but things were pretty hectic, so you might not remember her." He took the petite woman's hand, pulled her farther into the room and said, "Mom, this is Zena."

Esther placed her hand on her heart. She'd never seen him so happy. It was as clear as if he'd handed her a notarized declaration. At last, her prayers had been answered.

Joseph, I hope you're seeing this. Our son has

found his mate.

"Miss Zeeeeeena!" Eddy barreled into the petite woman and almost knocked her to the floor.

"Well, hey there." She laughed and hugged the kid. "Good to see you, too."

"You gotta see my room." The boy tugged at her hand and dragged her toward the back of the house. "It's so cool. I've got a huge comic book collection—and I found some beads on my bed this morning!"

A pang of nostalgia pricked at Jacob. It was like watching himself growing up again. He said in a low voice, "Not the good ones, right, Mom?"

Esther smiled. "No, I did not give him the first edition comics. You had a lot of doubles of the regular ones. He loves reading now, used to hate it."

"That's great," He gave her a hug. "He's lucky to have you. You knew how to hook him."

Daniel cleared his throat. "Hello, Jacob."

"Hey, Uncle Dan. Good to see you." He knew his mother wouldn't have invited him to dinner. Why was he here? "What's up? Everything okay?"

"You tell me. I'm going to funerals and you come rolling in the door looking like you're about to announce your engagement—" Daniel jerked his chin in the same direction Zena had gone "—to the little FBI agent."

Wind knocked out of him, Jacob could only say, "Excuse me?"

"We have four Indian women murdered, families grieving, and you're—what? Too busy with your new girlfriend to do your job?"

"Daniel, how dare you speak to Jacob that way? He's your brother's son—"

"My step-brother. But right now, I'm not speaking as an uncle." He turned his head to glare at the only other person in the room. "And I'm not talking to you, Esther."

Jacob closed the space between himself and his mother. "You've got something to say, you can say it in front of my mother." *You prick*. He'd never seen this side of the man before—or had he been naïve and oblivious to this side of his uncle? He was beginning to see why his mother loathed him.

"I'm the chairman, and the tribe pays your salary. Family or not, you're supposed to do your job. A lot of people have been coming to me, complaining about you, and how nothing is getting done." Daniel threw his hands up in the air. "What am I supposed to say? Go easy on the guy, he's new?"

Jacob gritted his teeth. "I'm not new. I have my degree in Criminal Justice, and I worked on the Billings PD for ten years before I came to work for the tribe."

"The job is new, and you haven't been in it that long. Maybe it's time to get someone who knows what they're doing."

"This case is a tough one—even for the feds. Everyone is working on it night and day." He took a deep breath and counted to ten. He wasn't about to beg for his job. He could get a job with the City of Billings or Yellowstone County in a heartbeat. "Besides which, the Tribal Council appointed me. You weren't alone in that decision."

Daniel sniffed. "Who do you think runs that group?" He stood and put his Stetson on. "I'll be calling a special meeting. You might want to attend—and bring your gun and badge with you so you can turn them in."

He headed toward the door and stopped. "That dinner invite is still open, Esther. Check your calendar. See if you're available this coming Saturday."

The door clicked shut, and Jacob released a long breath. "Mom, you're not going out to dinner with him, are you? I'll get another job."

"I've been telling that bastard no for years," Esther growled. "I have no intention of ever saying yes."

Flushed and smiling, Zena entered the kitchen. "Where'd Chairman Daniel go?"

"To hell, I hope," Esther snarled. "That jerk threatened Jacob's job."

The grin dropped off her face. "What?"

Jacob filled her in, making sure to include the thuggish attempt to force his mother to go out with him.

"Classy guy," Zena said. Her brow furrowed. "What was his job before he became involved in tribal politics? Mob enforcer?"

"Pest control," Esther responded. "He hated wearing the uniform and going out to people's homes to do menial work. Felt it was beneath him—he was too good to be an exterminator."

Jacob gaped. "I never knew that."

His mother shrugged. "You were a kid with PTSD, and you couldn't remember anything for six months after your father was murdered."

"Mrs. Graywolf—"

"Please, call me Esther." She patted Zena on the shoulder. "We're pretty informal."

Zena nodded and pointed at the table. "Did he—Chairman Daniel—drink out of that coffee cup?"

"Yes. Why?"

In a flash, Jacob saw exactly where she was going

with this. "Hang on." He grabbed a plastic bag out of a cabinet. "Put it in here. We'll take it to the lab."

"I want my mug back. It's part of a set," his mother said and stopped. "Wait. You think he's the killer?"

"Can't rule anyone out," Jacob said.

"Including a spurned suitor," Zena responded. "He's the invisible man, coming and going without being noted, part of the background."

"He was at the hospital the same day Mrs. Otterlegs died."

"At our meeting with the mayor, he said the killer was going old school with scalping the victims," Zena added.

Esther's hand flew to her chest. "Ohmigod."

"Don't say anything to anyone about this," Jacob warned. "Indian telegraph."

"In Summertown, we call that the Adalwolf grapevine," Zena said.

Jacob shook his head. "We might have to get rid of him."

A trembling little voice piped up from the hallway. "Are you guys talking about me?"

Esther rushed to Eddy and pulled him into a bear hug. "No, honey."

His skinny shoulders shook, and he sobbed into her neck, "Please don't send me away."

"Oh, Eddy, the only way I'm going to let you go is if you don't want to be here anymore."

Jacob's heart ached for the kid. If his father and mother had died that fateful night, he'd have been in Eddy's moccasins, a little waif shuttled from foster home to foster home, ending up God only knew where.

"Hey, Eddy," Jacob said. "I have some special

comic books signed by the artists. Would you like to see a first edition Captain Fantastic?"

The kid looked up, wiped his nose with his sleeve, and nodded.

"Good. I've been saving it for someone special. Someone like you."

Chapter Thirteen

Cowboy Motel~*~ Billings, Montana

Wearing a black hoodie over a plain T-shirt, and jeans, the Doctor rapped on number three's apartment door at the rundown motel. The door cracked open, and an orange-tinged eyeball stared at him. The old man slid the chain back, revealing a shabby room.

"You came," he croaked, disbelief mirrored in his voice and face. "I never thought I'd see you again."

The Doctor glanced over his shoulder. It was after sundown and he was dressed in dark clothing, but he had no interest in being spotted by a random prostitute or john stumbling around the parking lot. "Can I come in?"

"Please." The elder opened the door and stepped back. "Sorry, I'm in a state of shock. You're actually here."

The Doctor slid into the room and glanced around. Threadbare vomit green carpet. An orange countertop by the crappy bathroom area. A sagging queen-sized bed, no doubt crawling with bedbugs, squatted alongside a battered brown nightstand. Propped against the wall, an ancient TV with a sign indicating it was attached to a burglary system looked as if it wished it could vanish into the faux wood paneling. And a lone wooden chair stood by the heater.

The Doctor took a seat and crossed his ankles, his hands in the pockets of his hoodie. "Nice place," he said, without even attempting to hide the sarcasm in his voice.

"Cheap and crappy. Like me." His *pappy* shrugged and sat on the bed facing him. "You have every right to hate me."

"I do admit, I was very angry at you for many years." The Doctor nodded. "But you know who really pissed me off?"

His father shook his head, a bewildered expression on his face.

"Rose." He slapped his thigh with a palm. "My beautiful, hard-working mother who abandoned me not long after you disappeared."

The old man frowned. "Son, she *died*."

"A little too convenient, wouldn't you say?"

"You think she died on *purpose*?"

"She had a child—two children—to care for. She gave one up and kept her favorite. Me." He nodded, thinking back to those halcyon days when it was only him and his mother. The trips to the parks, visits to museums. Anything free that was open on her days off was fair game for their time together.

"I'm not following, son."

"Stop calling me son." The Doctor slammed his fist on the arm of the chair. "You were a sperm donor, nothing more."

"But she had heart disease—"

"Shut up. You worthless piece of shit. She had a *responsibility* to take care of herself, to be there for *me,* her chosen child. Any mother who truly cared for her child would train like an athlete to be there day and night for him."

The old man stood, shaky on his feet, and ran his fingers through his hair. "I don't understand. You're a Doctor. Why are you blaming her for her illness?"

"I hear this every freaking day from whiny bitches. 'I'm sick, I can't help it.' They can help it. They don't want to control their impulses."

His so-called father shuffled away from him toward the bathroom. "I have to use the toilet. Can't control my bladder anymore. Cancer." He turned the light on, and the vent fan came on.

"Alcohol and cancer. Smoking and cancer." The Doctor raised his voice to be heard over the exhaust. "Smoking and heart disease. Eating greasy cholesterol laden food. It's all out there for the public to see and learn. But do they stop drinking, smoking, and eating garbage? No—because they *can't help themselves.*"

Zipping his pants with a shaking hand, the old man shuffled over and stood in front of him. "I'm sorry I asked you here."

"She was *weak.* And she left me to rot in the foster care system, to be passed around like a piece of meat for predators." The Doctor trembled with rage. "She must *pay* for what she did to me."

"She's dead. There's nothing you can do to her now." His voice no longer hesitant, the sperm donor pointed at the door. "Go. I've heard enough."

The Doctor smirked but didn't budge. "I brought you a gift. Aren't you interested in seeing what it is?"

A tear trickled down a jaundiced cheek. "There's nothing left for me in this world, son, not even you."

The Doctor stood and gazed into the rheumy eyes of the man reeking of death and placed his hand on the elder's bony shoulder. "At least you accepted responsibility for your actions. More than I can say for my mother." He extended his peace offering, a white packet containing his favorite treatment. "You have a glass of water around? This will help you with the pain."

Surprise mixed with gratitude filled the old man's eyes, and he shuffled to the bathroom and returned with a grimy glass.

The Doctor stirred the powder into the liquid and handed it to the geezer. "Bottom's up."

Tears filled the orange-tinged eyes. "I don't know what to say."

The Doctor smiled. "Say good-bye."

****

A short while later, the Doctor drove his vehicle into the pool of darkness at the edge of the grocery store parking lot. Any moment now, that silly little cashier would be getting off work and coming right to him. He left the car running and watched the employees flowing out the front door. When she appeared in the circle of light at the exit, he tapped his horn. She squinted, waved, and smiled.

Come to papa. I've been thinking about you.

Things were falling into place nicely. He chuckled. Perhaps he should be giving out coupons. Tonight was a super twofer. First the disgusting old man, now this middle-aged woman. He never killed kids. They were young and vulnerable, like he'd been once.

The woman opened the door and hopped in. "I wasn't sure you'd show."

He reached over, pulled her close, and stroked her long black hair. *So silky. She took such good care of what God had given her.* He murmured, "Why would you say that?"

"A lot of guys flirt with me and then they ghost me." She gave him a shy smile. "Guess you're different."

"Oh, yes," he agreed. "I'm not one of those no-shows." He put the car in gear. "Let's go somewhere private so we can discuss your aches and pains."

She placed her hand on his knee and slid it up his thigh. "Maybe we can talk about something else."

Against his wishes, his groin stirred to life, demanding attention. *That wouldn't do.* One hand on the wheel, he pushed her wandering digits aside. "Not now. You don't want me to be a distracted driver, do you?"

Giggling, she unzipped her parka, revealing she was naked from the waist up. "I plan to distract you a lot."

While not immune to the beauty of her perky breasts and eraser hard nipples, he had no intention of having sex with this woman. *No.* That was a distinctly different type of partner.

"You're getting cold. You better cover those up."

Closing the jacket, she pouted. "Didn't you say you could fix my pain? Sex always helps my back aches."

"I'm sure it does." A short while later, he pulled into the parking lot behind a burnt-out hulk of a building. "Now, turn around, take off your jacket, and let me see your back."

She dropped her jacket, and he ran his hands down her back.

"That feels nice," she cooed.

Leaning his head against hers, he inhaled the herbal

scent of her shampoo. "Your hair is lovely," he breathed and slid her locks to one side. "You take good care of it."

She squirmed in an attempt to turn around, but he gripped her arms to keep her in place. She began to struggle, and panic filled her voice. "You're hurting me."

"This will only take a moment," the Doctor intoned.

Wriggling one arm free, she reached up and her fingers dug at his hand. "Stop. I'm not into kinky sex."

"Neither am I—at least not with you."

Chapter Fourteen

Hotel LaBelle ~*~ Billings, Montana

Bright and early on Saturday morning, Jacob arrived at the Hotel LaBelle for a hastily convened meeting with Zena, Tallulah, and Bronco. The tantalizing aroma of bacon lingered in the air, and Jacob wondered if it would be rude to ask for a bite to eat. He and Zena had been out most of the night in wolf form, searching for any additional clues at Mrs. Otterlegs' home, to no avail. If *only* they had something with a fingerprint or a trace of DNA from the victims' homes to tie the crimes to one killer. After spending half the night sniffing at every cubic inch of the cluttered home, they'd given up. The only people they tracked were Mrs. Otterlegs, Eddy—and each other. Much as their animal urges had called to them like a siren's song, their rational human side had prevailed.

As he shook Lucius' hand, Jacob's stomach growled. "Sorry, long night. No time to grab breakfast."

"Well shoot. You don't have to say that twice." He turned and bellowed, "Tallulah, throw some more grub on the table. The wolves are starving."

Jacob shook his head. "Subtlety is not your forte, my friend."

"If you don't A.S.K. you don't G.E.T." Lucius led the way into the kitchen. "Your gal has chowed down

133

twice her weight in pancakes and eggs. Even Bronco is in awe—and that guy can *eat*."

Mid-bite, Zena raised a hand in greeting.

Next to her sat one of Jacob's related-by-marriage cousins, Bronco Winchester. At six-foot-two-inches, a little over two-hundred pounds, with long dark hair pulled back into a ponytail, he looked like a bad guy you'd cross the street to avoid. Except he worked for Bert in the Anomaly Defense Division, which put him in the good guy category.

Bronco stood and extended a big hand. "Good to see you, bro'. I hear you and Zena were out all night." He grinned. "If I didn't know you were such a Boy Scout, I'd accuse you two of doing the horizontal mambo."

Heat blazed in Jacob's face, and Zena started choking.

Bronco slapped her on the back. "No need to wolf your food. Tallulah has more."

Zena gasped and said, "Water went down the wrong pipe."

"Sure." Bronco quirked an eyebrow. "I'll pretend I haven't been keeping my hands away from your face for the last twenty minutes."

Tallulah placed a fresh platter of pancakes and sausages on the table in front of the big guy. "Where's your side kick?"

"He was doing a little hunting." Bronco poured syrup over a pile of pancakes. "He's on the steps, waiting to be invited in."

Jacob warned Zena, "Cover your ears."

She swallowed and said, "Why?"

Tallulah opened the kitchen door. A beautiful

bobcat strolled in, and a shrieking beige and black sphere streaked into the room.

"Omigod," Zena shouted. "Grab Franny. That cat will kill her."

Jacob slid into the seat next to hers, grabbed her hand, and said, "Watch."

The cat stood its ground, not backing down, but not going after the dog, either. Franny skidded to a halt, stood on her hind legs, and danced in front of the cat, her shrieks subsiding to yips. The cat plopped down at Bronco's feet, flicking his tail as the dog leaped on him and began to lick the feline as if he were a popsicle.

"Zena, meet Gaucho," Bronco said with a grin. "He's my partner. We're telepathically connected."

She shook her head. "A supernatural ugly little man. A ghost who leaves me eagle feathers—and now this?"

Jacob laughed. "Stick around, there's more. A *lot* more."

Bronco sat back and patted his stomach. "Thanks for breakfast. Now, what am I doing here?"

Tallulah pulled a chair out and sat with her hands folded on her belly. "I think these two need some help with a case, if I'm not mistaken."

Lucius finished removing the dishes from the table and placed them in the dishwasher. "I'm going to go check on Miriam. I left her coloring and watching cartoons in the saloon. If you need me for anything, holler."

Jacob pulled a printout of a headshot from his back pocket. "This is the guy I'd like you to follow via remote viewing. We have his address in Billings to give you a starting point. We'd like you to see what he's up to."

Tallulah studied the photo. "He looks like a teddy bear." She slid the paper over to Bronco.

"Appearances can be deceiving," Bronco said with a shrug. "Look at us."

"Who is he?" Tallulah asked.

"One of the new guys at Indian Health Services. Yesterday, he made some statements that could be construed as threats to himself and others. His name is Dr. Robert Mann."

A woman stepped into the kitchen, and the room erupted into a chorus of greetings. Swooping down to hug and kiss Tallulah and Bronco in turn, the six-foot-tall, designer suit attired female showered them with kisses. "Hello, handsome," she said, and pecked Jacob on the cheek. "Long time, no see. Great to see you and your pixie friend again."

Zena waved her fork up and down Stephanie's tall figure. "You are the best dressed woman I've ever met."

"Thank you. You're too sweet." The tall woman inspected Zena, looked at Jacob, then back again at Zena. "When's the wedding?"

Jacob dragged his hands down his face and groaned. "This is why I can't have nice things."

Stephanie snapped her fingers. "Honey, this woman's aura is *vibrating*. You'd better not wait too long. She might explode."

"Thanks." Jacob rolled his eyes. "We're kind of in the middle of something here, if you don't mind."

"M'kay," Stephanie said and tapped the photo. "Dr. Bob was at the Garrett with Rod and me last night. He arrived drunk. Had a bandage on his hand, made me think he might have gotten into a fight. We plied him with coffee, called a cab, and sent him home."

"Did he say anything that concerned you?" Zena broke in. "Like he might hurt himself or someone else?"

"He was *heartbroken*. Wouldn't go into detail, cried like a baby, and kept repeating that it was all his fault. He's been a regular at our place since summer. Arrives alone, has dinner, enjoys the show, and leaves alone. Never seen him this messed up. Rod and I figured it had to be man trouble."

Lucius galloped into the kitchen and screeched to a stop. "Turn on the news. There's something you gotta see."

An earnest looking woman in a black coat and scarf held a microphone and stared into the camera as the wind whipped her long dark hair. "A man said he was out walking his dog and the animal became agitated and slipped his leash. The dog led him to the body of a Native American woman in the burned-out Big Timber Lumber building. The Billings Police Department is asking for anyone who might have seen anything unusual in the area to call in on the dedicated tip line at 888-BPD-TIPS. Back to you, Tom."

The handsome news anchor gazed out at the TV audience with a somber expression. "Thanks, Tammy. We go now to a live interview with Chairman Daniel Redhawk at Crow Agency."

The flat screen TV in the kitchen filled with his uncle's scar-ravaged face. His face twisted with anger, Redhawk held his fist up as he spoke.

"For too long, we have been at the mercy of the federal government. Thanks to the Supreme Court, we have no ability to go after white men who kill our women. We are sick and tired of the murders of our woman—and now we have a serial killer in our midst."

"Oh, no," Zena gasped. "He's done it now."

"Dammit!" Jacob slammed his palm on the kitchen table. "That was not supposed to leave the conference room,"

Glaring at the camera, Daniel continued, "When we hired our own Tribal Chief of Police, we assumed things would be better. We'd be the masters of our own fate. But it looks like he has no interest in solving these heinous crimes. I'm calling an emergency Tribal Council Meeting to be held on Monday evening to discuss this crisis and to determine if it's time to terminate the employment of Jacob Graywolf. It will be an open meeting and members of the press are welcome to attend."

"What are you going to do?" Zena asked.

"It's easy to spew bullshit into a microphone when no one disagrees with you." Crossing his arms over his chest, he growled, "He said it's an open meeting. Let's see how he deals with the people who have the facts and are actually doing the work on this case—not just acting like they are."

****

Crow Reservation

Heart racing, mouth dry, Esther stood stock still in the garden on Saturday morning. She and Eddy had been gathering gourds, pumpkins, and other winter vegetables when Joseph appeared—again. Last night when he had appeared while she slept, he'd been laughing and dancing with her—until he'd morphed into a bloody statue. She'd woken up, hoping it had been a nightmare, an accumulation of the months' worth of stressors—and horrors. His absence in her bedroom seemed to confirm that it had only been a dream—until now.

No. Not again. Blood dripping, eyes beseeching, he floated above the cabbage plants. Tears blurred her vision. *Joseph, what am I to do?*

Eddy bounced to her side, Jessie chuffing and shuffling behind him. He held out a long yellow and green striped gourd. "Look at this long wriggly one. Doesn't it look like a snake?"

Esther looked at the boy, not actually seeing him, only seeing her beloved floating behind him.

"Who's Joseph?" Eddy asked.

Startled, she pulled her gaze away from her husband's ghost and stared at Eddy. "What?"

"You keep saying, 'Joseph, Joseph, Joseph.' Who is he?" The boy cocked his head. "Are you okay?"

She was positive she hadn't spoken out loud. "Was I talking?"

Eddy looked down and dragged his foot in the earth. "Not with your lips. With your mind."

Kneeling at his level, she placed a knuckle under his chin and gently lifted his head to look him in the eyes. "Is this a practical joke?"

Tears welled in his eyes, and he shook his head. "No." His lower lip trembled. "The only other person who knows I hear voices is my mother—and she's dead."

Esther hugged him. "I'm so sorry. I was thinking about my husband, Joseph." She took a deep, shuddering breath. "He died when Jacob was your age."

"I'm sorry." The boy snuffled in her shoulder. "I

didn't mean to upset you."

"I was surprised." Shocked was probably the right word, but the boy looked terrified, and she didn't want to scare him further. "How long have you been hearing people's thoughts?"

"All my life." He shrugged. "When I learned to talk, my mom said I would answer people. She said it was funny at first. My mom told me to keep it a secret. People would think I was crazy, take me away, and lock me up."

She sighed. "Your mom was right." She stood up and yanked off her leather gardening gloves. "What else did she tell you?"

"She said it was a gift and that strong medicine men and women had it."

Esther nodded. "It's called clairaudience, which is a fancy word for hearing clearly, or hearing thoughts. Did she work with you to control your gift?"

"Yeah, she told me to sing a song in my head, and it would help block out the voices. And to stay away from big crowds until I'm old enough to tune them out. She bought me an MP3 player so I could listen to music, and it helped."

"What about school?"

"It was bad. I'm not allowed to wear my earbuds in class, and I couldn't get the other kids out of my head." He shrugged. "It's better now. They want to read my comic books, so they're being very nice to me. The teachers, too."

"So, before, you'd hear them thinking and get angry and get in trouble, is that right?"

"Yeah." He looked sad. "With all the moves, I lost my MP3 player. It's quiet here, and your thoughts are nice, so it's been good. I wish my mom could see how much better I'm doing now."

"I'm sure she's watching, and she's very proud. I'm betting we can find another device for you." She put her arm around his shoulder. "How about a snack break?"

He grinned. "Yes, that'd be great."

Joseph floated beside Eddy, blood dripping down his arms, past his waist now.

"I need to make a phone call to Jacob."

Eddy's smile faltered, and alarm rippled across his face. "About me?"

She pulled him into a side hug. "About Joseph. You were right. He's very much on my mind."

He held up his prize vegetable. "Can I take this to school?"

"Yes, absolutely. Now go wash your hands. I have oatmeal cookies to go with our hot cocoa."

Humming a little tune, he skipped into the house. She followed the boy—however, there was no joy in her steps. She dreaded calling her son. When his phone went to voicemail, guilt-tinged relief surged through her.

"Honey, your father dropped by again. Call me, please. I have something else I need to share with you." *A nine-year-old kid who can read minds, to be exact.*

Esther put the milk on the stove and pulled the superhero cookie jar off the shelf. She wondered how much of her self-talk Eddy had been overhearing. Esther's mind was a continuous internal dialogue. *Do this, not that. Make sure the stethoscope is warm. I need to go to the store, get some milk, eggs, cheese. I wonder if that new place is open.*

It's a wonder the poor kid hadn't had a meltdown under the strain of all her mental chatter alone, much less that of other people. When Eddy first arrived, he'd been adamant that Wanda wanted him out of her house. Tommy had denied that his wife had ever said such a thing, but this experience made her rethink her assumptions.

"Aunt Esther?" Eddy came into the kitchen.

"Yes?" She measured sugar and cocoa into the boiling milk and began to swirl the ingredients together.

He sat at the table and pried the lid off the jar. "Can I tell you something?"

"Of course."

"I don't like Mr. Daniel." He chomped into a cookie. "He has bad thoughts."

She froze mid-stir. "Why do you say that?"

"When he was here the other night, he kept thinking over and over, 'I'm glad he's dead, I'm glad he's dead.' "

The hot cocoa boiled over, and she snapped the burner off. *That bastard.*

"My mom would've washed my mouth out with soap if I used that word."

"That's the least of my bad language for that man." Esther ground her teeth. "Maybe you can give me a pass when it comes to Mr. Daniel. I have many more words I'd like to use on him—but I'm saving them all for a special occasion."

Chapter Fifteen

Yellowstone County Medical Examiner and Coroner's Office
Billings, Montana

Joe greeted Zena and Jacob at the door of the county morgue. He glanced at his watch. "Almost midnight on a Sunday. You guys do know there's only two of us, the mortuary technician and me, right? He gets OT. I don't."

"It's on Hal's budget, not mine," Jacob deadpanned.

"Nor mine," Zena added.

"The least you could do is give me the whiskey you promised me." He shook his head. "I work, and I work, but does anyone ever thank me—"

"Here." Zena thrust out a brown paper bag. "Happy now?"

Joe peeked into the bag and gave her a toothy grin. "Yes, ma'am, I am. Twenty-five years and in a wooden box, no less. You know how to treat a guy right." He swept off an imaginary hat and bowed. "Come right in."

As they walked through the doors, the acrid smell of cleaning solution burned Zena's nose and eyes. She'd adjust to it—eventually.

Jacob rubbed his hands together, cupped them

together, and then blew air over the joined fists. "Is the county cutting back on heat?"

"No." Joe pointed to a collection of blue gowns. "Grab one of those, along with gloves and masks." He stretched a pair of nitrile gloves over his large hands. "You'll thank me for the meat locker temps when I open one of these drawers." He handed Zena a jar of mentholated petroleum jelly. "You'll want this. Mouth breathing ain't gonna cut it."

She smeared the aromatic ointment under her nose and passed the container to Jacob before hooking the mask over her ears. "The woman was found in an empty building in freezing temperatures. How bad could she smell?"

"Not her." Joe snapped open a stainless-steel door and pulled out a long drawer. "Him."

A miasma of urine, feces, and decay filled the room like a toxic cloud, and Zena gagged. "Road kill smells better than this."

"You're not wrong," Joe agreed. "We'll clean him up all nice and proper for the funeral home director, but not until we're done."

Wincing, Jacob asked, "Who is this? What does he have to do with the woman we came to see?"

"As to the who, all we know is he's some guy a clerk found in room three of the Cowboy Motel. The people in the next room called this morning to complain about the weird smells coming through the bathroom vent. The TV was on, so they knocked on the door, got no answer. The clerk used his key and got a nasty surprise." Joe pointed at the elderly man on the metal table with the jaundiced skin and orange eyes. "The heat in the room had been left on full blast, like an easy bake oven, which accelerated the decomp—in addition to his disease already taking its toll on him. I took a peek under the hood this afternoon, since we have a rush on autopsies these days. Pancreatic cancer. Nasty stuff. He was dying."

"Any ID?" Zena held her arm over her face, but the stench oozed under the mask and into every nook and cranny of her nose and the room.

"At the No Tell Motel?" Joe chuckled and shook his head. "Guy paid with cash, no wallet, not even a receipt found in the room. You can ask the detectives, but when I got there, the cops on the scene said it looked like the room had been tossed. They believed it was a robbery gone wrong."

Jacob took the words out of her mouth. "You're thinking it *wasn't* a break in?"

The ME nodded. "Whoever did this was trying to use heat to accelerate the body's decomposition, maybe hide the time of death—and to cover up something else."

Exasperated, Zena threw her hands up. "Stop teasing us."

"All right, all right." Joe reached for a sheaf of print outs and handed them to her. "I put a rush on the tox screen for stomach contents, blood serum, and vitreous fluid from the eyeball. You can put me on your holiday shopping list for a case of that single-malt scotch."

Zena and Jacob studied the lab results together. "Shit," she breathed. "The same frigging poison, brucine." She glanced up at the corpse. "Why isn't he curled back like a pretzel?"

"Because, my little FBI pixie—" the gray-haired

ME waved at the elderly man "—heat accelerates muscle relaxation—and in this case, the signs of the poison."

"This is unexpected," Zena murmured. "An old woman, an old man, neither fit his profile."

"No long black hair on this guy," Jacob said. "Scalp wounds?"

Joe pulled the old man's lank yellow-white hair up from the side of his neck. "The worst of the bunch. Almost looks like he was trying to rip his head off."

Zena cringed at the size of the ragged wound, the biggest of all the ones they had seen so far. "If the perp was trying to cover up and make this look like he didn't do it, he failed miserably. This almost looks like the killer tore it off with his fingernails in a fit of rage. Was Mr. Doe alive or dead when it happened?"

"No bruising, not a lot of blood on the carpet at the scene, so his heart wasn't pumping."

"Small mercies," Jacob said with a sigh. "Still vicious. Makes you wonder if he died before the killer wanted."

"All this John Doe needed was a tiny push. The angel of death was flapping his wings nearby, anyway. My guess is the killer miscalculated how fast the poison would work on him in his debilitated condition."

Zena sighed. "What about the female victim? Do we have a name?"

Joe returned Mr. Doe to the bowels of the chiller and opened the next one. "Darla Birdsong, single, age thirty-three, clerk at the Organic Grocery Store. Found nude from the waist up under her parka."

Zena gazed at the young woman with the sheet draped across her chest. Her head was arched back, and her hands curled in awkward positions. "So young."

"I know her family," Jacob said in a soft voice. "She moved to Billings to be closer to work. Any signs of sexual assault?"

"Nope, and her stomach didn't tell us anything," Joe said. "However, the tox screen matched our male victim. There's a new twist in this guy's MO." He pulled her long black hair away from her neck. "This scalp wound is not as large as the old guy's, but he didn't bother sewing it up. Up until this old man and this young woman, he's always sewn up the wound on the bodies I've autopsied. Makes me think he might have been in a hurry."

Jacob and Zena bumped heads getting a closer look at the cut. She rubbed her head. "Watch it, buster."

"Ahem," Joe interrupted. "I'm giving you a lesson here."

"Yes, sir," Jacob said, and waggled his eyebrows at her.

"I found a puncture wound by her jugular, an injection site." Joe held his hands out like a magician. "Death would have been almost instantaneous."

"Because he wasn't creepy enough, he had to up the ante with injections?" Jacob grimaced. "Sick dude."

"Pervy and smart. I had hoped she might have saved some tissue for us under her nails—or elsewhere. Nada. The perp was careful," Joe agreed. "One of these is like the other, one of these is kinda the same. Both Darla and John Doe died from brucine. He wanted to cover up the old guy's death and not hers."

Zena mused. "This old guy holds a secret. Maybe we can unlock it with—"

"DNA," Jacob finished her sentence.

Grinning, Joe handed Zena another piece of paper. "This is a request for urgent assistance from the FBI's DNA Database. You wouldn't happen to know someone who could help us get this expedited, would you?"

"You're the best." She pulled Joe in for a sideways hug. "I'm on it."

As she turned to leave with Jacob, the ME called out, "Not that I'm complaining, but next time would it kill you to throw a kiss in, too?"

****

Two days after his glorious double killing, the Doctor made his way to his apartment with his groceries in hand from the twenty-four-hour convenience store. As he put his key in the door, a woman spoke.

"Well, fancy meeting you here." Mary Longbow, the middle-aged LPN who worked in the clinic leaned against a hallway wall with a big smile on her face.

"It's late. What brings you here?" He turned the key but didn't open the door.

"I happened to be in the neighborhood." She fluttered her eyelashes. "I wondered what the doctors' living quarters were like."

"Very vanilla, nothing special." He was not about to invite her in. *Don't shit where you eat.*

She laughed—a low, throaty chuckle that made him cringe. "I hope you don't think I'm being too forward, but a couple of people at work told me you're gay. I told them you hadn't met the right woman."

This old cow was trying to bed him? He could have anyone he wanted. Why would he pick her? The idea of having sex with her made his stomach roil.

"Mary," he said using a tone he reserved for children, "have you been drinking?"

Eyes twinkling, she giggled and played with her long black hair. "Shhh," her voice slurred. "Don't tell anyone. No booze allowed on the reservation."

"Yes, well, I'm sure there's a good reason for that." *Like a rampant problem with alcoholism, for starters.* "You shouldn't be driving. Do you have a ride home?"

"I got nothing to go home to. Kids are all grown up, moved away. No dogs, not even a cat." She took two wobbly steps closer to him. "Maybe I could stay with you?" She pointed to a large purse sitting on the floor. "I've got everything I need, even a toothbrush."

He *had* to get rid of this woman.

"Are those the same scrubs you wore on Friday?" *Did she even bathe?*

Surprised, she looked down. "Of course not. They all look the same. It's easier to wear the same uniform every day." Her eyes narrowed. "You think I'm dirty?"

"No, not at all," he lied. "I like to change out of my scrubs before I go home."

She picked up her bag. "So, can I come in?"

He pondered the situation. If he left her in the hall, she might create a scene and attract unwanted attention. If he let her into his apartment, would she pass out? She seemed woozy. Maybe that was the better choice. Put her on the sofa, let her sleep it off, and go back to work tomorrow. She'd probably be mortified when she woke up. And beg him to keep it a secret.

"Okay." He pushed the door open and hoisted his groceries. "You can sleep on the couch. Tomorrow morning you and I will go back to work. We will never speak of this. It will be our little secret."

"I'm good at keeping secrets," she whispered and ran her fingernail down his back. "Like the day that old guy came, and you rushed him into the administrator's office, I never said a word."

Heart in his throat, not trusting himself to speak, he put the cans and boxes of food away in the galley kitchen cupboards with exaggerated care. Now he *truly* had to get rid of this woman. *Permanently.*

"Pardon me?" he breathed. "What old man?"

"The guy who looked like an orange, that one. Not an Indian, that's for sure. Whiter than white once upon a time." Mary laughed and sank onto the beige sofa. "He sure had you all shook up. You were *pissed.*"

Attempting to control his anger, he took a long, deep breath. "Ah, him. An old family friend. And yes, I was angry at him. He was his own worst enemy, drank himself into that state." He neglected to mention the pancreatic cancer. She didn't need to know. In fact, she shouldn't have known anything at all. "So, tell me. Have you been spying on me, Mary?"

"I'm observant, I notice things." A sly look crossed her face. "You're an attractive man. Why shouldn't I watch you? Is there a law against that?"

He gave her his most winsome smile and sat next to her. "I'm flattered." He stroked her head. "You have the loveliest hair, did you know that?"

She reached up to pull his lips to hers. "I want you."

"And I want you." He stood. "But not like this. I don't want you to wake up in the morning and feel like I took advantage of you because you'd been drinking."

Mary's lower lip quivered, and a tear rolled down

her cheek. "You think I'm old and fat and ugly."

He grabbed her hand and kissed her knuckles. "Not at all. I want you to enjoy it when we are together—soon. It's not enjoyable for me if it's not fun for you."

Nodding slowly, she said in a small voice, "Okay."

"Good. Not a word to anyone about this, right? I wouldn't want to get you into trouble. If asked and I told someone you showed up drunk here tonight and tried to seduce me, you could lose your job."

Panic filled her eyes. "No, no. Not a word. It's our secret. I swear."

"I'm glad we understand each other. We'll have a real date in a special place, I promise. Sweet dreams."

No sleep for him. He had to make a plan to get rid of this woman—and soon.

Chapter Sixteen

Multi-Purpose   Building   ~*~   Crow   Agency,
Montana

Jacob jostled for a place in the meeting room on
Monday evening, pulling Zena and Esther behind him
in his wake. The municipal planners had *never* expected
this large a group for this space. He glanced around,
searching for Tommy Otterlegs, and spotted the fire
marshal lounging against a back wall, eying the crowd.
Like a salmon swimming upstream, Jacob wriggled
between attendees, each of them intent on shaking his
hand and whispering words of encouragement. Behind
him, the same people greeted his mother with loud
hellos. When he glanced back, Zena was right behind
him, but his mother was enveloped in a bear hug by a
large man. He wasn't surprised by the outpouring of
affection for his mom. She'd been delivering babies on
the rez for three decades. He was shocked, however, by
the continuous stream of support—for him.

The fire marshal, Abe Runs Strong, an old high
school friend, quirked an eyebrow at him. "You do
this?"

"No, you can thank Redhawk for this mess. But
I'm sure he'd like to blame me for all the tribe's ills,
including this pow-wow. All we need is the dancing
and drumming and we'll have the annual fair."

"I've been counting heads." Abe lifted his chin. "We're already over the maximum number of people in the room."

"What's your plan?"

Abe pointed at the folding walls. "The guys are working on opening those to expand the area. After that, we're going to have to tell people to take turns coming in."

If it came to that, some members of the tribe would think the council was doing things in secret, hiding nefarious goings on. "That will not go over well."

"Trust me, I know. Let's hope I don't have to."

A microphone squealed, and a gavel rapped. Those who could find seats took them. Others stood along the walls, most with their arms crossed over their chests. The roar of the crowd subsided to a simmering rumble.

Zena and his mother finally made it to his side. He introduced the little redhead to Abe—who favored Jacob with a look from high school, the one that said, 'Hot babe.' If Jacob hadn't been so tense about the possibility of losing his job, he would have laughed out loud. *Hot babe, indeed.*

"Settle down, everyone. Settle *down.*" Redhawk struck the wooden hammer again—and the head flew out into the crowd.

From the back of the room someone yelled, "You first, Chairman."

The scars on his face and neck filled with color, and his lips thinned into a straight line. "We are here to discuss a serious issue, the safety of our tribe—or the lack of it under the current leadership. We are here to discuss the removal of Tribal Police Chief Graywolf from his job."

The rumble grew louder, and he raised his voice to be heard over the muttering and grumbling.

"Jacob Graywolf has failed to serve and protect this community." He lifted a sheaf of documents. "I have here in my hand numerous complaints about the performance of his duties."

"That looks like a stack of blank forms," a woman close to the front of the room yelled. "Show them to us."

"That would be violating confidentiality." The volume of the protests grew, and he put the microphone closer to his mouth. "These people fear reprisal."

"Who?" another woman demanded. "Drunk drivers? Meth dealers? Petty thieves? Isn't that why he's here? To protect us?"

Looking straight at Jacob, he spat out, "Ask *him* why he hasn't stopped a *serial killer*."

A collective gasp sucked all the air out of the room and all eyes turned to Jacob. His uncle smirked at him, his face glowing with triumph. Gotcha, he mouthed at his nephew.

"Serial killer?" The words ricocheted around the room, moving from lips to lips, shocked expressions turning to fear and anger.

"Yeah," his uncle said in a growl. "A serial killer, right here on our reservation and in our city. And that guy—" he nodded at Jacob "—and his girlfriend, the FBI agent, have been doing nothing. Maybe he's been too *distracted* to do his job."

Jacob retorted, "That is neither accurate nor appropriate." He turned to Zena for support, but she wasn't paying attention to the uproar in the room.

She stared at her cell phone, tapped a few keys, and

slid it into her pocket. Grabbing both Esther and Jacob by the arms, she surprised him with the strength of her grip. "I need you two to come with me."

"What the hell are you doing?" Jacob protested. "I'm in the middle of the fight of my life and you're doing what? Helping him destroy me?"

She shook her head. "Not now."

Tugging at them in earnest, she dragged the two of them through the closest exit.

"Has there been a break in the case? Did they find that sick bastard?"

Silent, she clamped her hand on his arm tighter and continued to tow them, like a horse dragging a travois laden with household goods. The more he tried to shake her off, the harder she gripped.

"What the hell is going on?"

Behind them, his uncle roared, "Run, chicken little, run. You coward. Everyone sees you for who you are now. She leads you around by the nose, while neither you nor she are helping your people. You're a disgrace, not fit to wear the badge."

Suddenly, he realized her scent had changed from her usual woodsy scent to a pungent, urgent, wild one. She was usually so open with him, so outgoing—but this demeanor was wrong. It was one she might use when arresting someone. He spoke only for her ears. "Are you arresting me?"

She dragged them into the outer lobby and pointed to a row of utilitarian plastic chairs. "Take a seat."

Staring off into the distance, his mother whispered, "Oh, Joseph, what has your brother done?"

Great. Even my dead father is here for this debacle.

Esther began to pray. *"Baruch atah Adonai Eloheinu, Melech haolam—"*

The front doors blew open, arctic air blasted through the lobby, and a small army of men and women in blue jackets emblazoned with FBI in large yellow letters swarmed in.

"I couldn't say anything until now. I'm sorry."

He stared at the show of force marching past them through the lobby and into the meeting room.

Squatting in front of them, Zena grabbed each of their hands. "This is about your father, Jacob—your husband, Esther."

In the adjacent meeting room, someone yelled, "FBI, everyone stay put."

She took a deep breath and let it out in a slow hiss. "Twenty-four years ago, Joseph Graywolf was murdered, and no clues were found—except those locked in your mind."

A tunnel of darkness overtook Jacob, allowing in ambient sounds, but blocking his vision, forcing him to watch time unfold before his eyes.

Suddenly he was nine years old again, in his wolf form, and out for a run with his father on a beautiful night. It wasn't their first time out, but it was an important night—his birthday. They hadn't gotten far from the house, no more than a half-mile, getting into the loping rhythm he loved.

In the distance, the murmur of the crowd rose, the noise of a river turning into a waterfall. The building shook with the stomping of feet—

Tiger swooped down in front of them.

A man shouted over the crowd, "FBI. We have a warrant for the arrest of Daniel Redhawk."

His father snapped, "That's the messenger of death. Go, hide, say nothing. NOW." A nearby thicket of bushes offered Jacob cover. He didn't know what was about to happen, but his father's scent had gone from playful to panicked—and that was enough proof for him that something terrible was coming.

The microphone reverberated with his uncle's shout, "What do you think you're doing? Get away from me. You're on tribal lands. You have no authority here."

Shaking with fear, but anxious to see what was happening, he peeked between the branches.

"*Someone*—get these people away from me. Get the Chief of Police back in here—he should be protecting me!"

His father crouched ready to spring at—what?

The microphone clattered and shrieked.

Tiger's scream echoed through the night.

His uncle's voice rose above the crowd's questions. "Take these handcuffs off me right now."

A dark figure backlit by the full moon battled with Tiger, screaming at the owl to get away.

Suddenly, his uncle stood in front of him, shouting obscenities. "You worthless bastard! You and your witch of a mother did this to me. I'll sue you. I'll take you down!"

His uncle stood in front of his father, a handgun pointed at him, taunting him. "You got the girl, you got to be Chief, what did I get? Nothing, nothing, and nothing. You were always the favorite, the chosen one. You were the one who could become a wolf. I was the ugly stepson, the one without any special abilities, the dud. I was supposed to be so grateful to your father for marrying my mother and taking us in—but I hated him and you. I've been waiting for this day all my life. This time I win." Snarling, *his father leaped, snapping, biting, and slashing at the little man consumed with jealous rage.*

The front door slammed open.

The gun went off and Jacob's father buckled to the ground.

Panting, Daniel Redhawk cried out with a hoarse voice, "Nooooo!"

His father began transforming back into his human form, and his uncle shrieked, "Noooooo! You were supposed to stay in your wolf form. You were supposed to be a wolf killed by a hunter. Dammit, Joseph, you screwed everything up. I'm supposed to be in charge, and I'm supposed to marry Esther. You've ruined everything. This is all your fault."

His uncle screamed, "Damn you, Jacob, this is all your fault!"

Too shaken to move or speak, Jacob stayed in the bushes until his mother found him the next morning, naked and trembling, crying silently, speaking not a word, like his father had said.

His mother's voice broke through his fugue state. "Jacob, can you hear me? They arrested your uncle for the murder of your father."

Vision blurred, mouth sticky with years of silence, he nodded. "I remember now. I remember that horrible night when he murdered Dad. He's a monster."

"He's the sociopath who followed the rule to keep your friends close and your enemies closer. Redhawk wasn't sure how much either of you might suspect him. He pretended to be the good uncle to keep tabs on you and your mother. Plus, he still wanted Esther for himself." She took his hand in hers. "The case was cold, but your father kept the evidence on his body, under his nails. It was there all along, waiting for technology to catch up." She paused and smiled. "Esther makes a mean cup of coffee—strong enough to catch a killer."

Chapter Seventeen

Crow Indian Health Service ~*~ Crow Agency, Montana

Two weeks after her brother-in-law was arrested, Esther sat in her car outside the clinic and took a long, deep breath. She was ready, had to be ready to go back to work, to face this head on. As she'd told the grief counselor, she wasn't afraid people wouldn't be supportive. No, she dreaded the whispers and pitying glances from friends and strangers alike. Discovering Daniel had murdered her husband had given her closure, of a sort—but had opened the wound she'd worked hard to heal. Reliving his death was like losing him all over again—without the constant stream of mourners and casseroles.

"You can do this, Esther," she said to her reflection in the rearview mirror. "You come from strong stock, Holocaust survivors. Your mother and aunt were little kids and they made it out of the concentration camps. *Buck up.* Don't be a wimp. Do it for your son, your husband, yourself."

Esther put her head down on the steering wheel and sobbed. The therapist said there was no set timeline for grief. Everyone was different—but few had a husband murdered by their brother-in-law. *Daniel.* That rattlesnake.

A hand came down on her right shoulder and squeezed. She jerked and turned in her seat.

"Joseph—omigod. You're here—and not gushing blood."

His expression was one of concern—mixed with affection.

Tears spilled down her cheeks, and her breath caught in hiccups of sobs. "What am I supposed to do?"

For the first time in all his visits, he spoke in a low, soft voice. "I love you and will always be here for you. Esther, you must live so others may live, too."

He bowed his head and kissed her on the lips. He tasted like summer filled with sunshine, mountain air, and huckleberries. Closing her eyes, she wished the kiss would last a lifetime. She blinked, opened her mouth to tell him that—and he was gone, leaving a scent of falling leaves behind.

Dabbing her eyes, Esther opened the car door and marched into the clinic with her head held high.

As she entered, a murmur filled the room, then a chant, "Esther, Esther, Esther." Everyone in the clinic, doctors, nurses, and patients, stood clapping their hands and smiling.

Frances Deerfoot, pushing a stroller swaddled with a blue blanket, was the first to embrace her. "Welcome back. We need you here."

Wiping her eyes with the heels of her hand, Esther squatted to coo at the bright-eyed infant she had delivered. "Such a beautiful boy. What did you name him?"

"Joseph," Frances said in a low voice. "We can only hope that he grows up to be half the man your husband was."

Sharon Buchbinder

Her vision blurry, voice hoarse, Esther replied, "With you as his mother, he's destined to be great." She stood and hugged Frances. "The tribe is so lucky to have you as the new chairman." She laughed. "You'll whip the men on the council into shape in no time."

"From your lips to the Creator's ears." Frances sighed. "There's some *we've always done it this way* stuff going on, but we'll work through it." She shook her head. "I'm going to have the medicine woman cleanse the meeting room with sage. Rid it of Redhawk's presence."

"That's a great idea," Esther said. "I'll get her out to my house, too."

"I'll let you get back to work." Frances inclined her head to the side. "You have a waiting room full of mothers who need to see you."

Esther turned and Mary Longbow flung herself onto her neck.

"Oh, thank God you're back. We've all been so worried about you," the LPN exclaimed. "This place has been like a morgue without you." She gasped and put her hand over her mouth. "I'm so sorry. I'm an idiot."

"You don't have to walk on eggshells around me. I'm not that fragile. I won't break." She patted the other woman's hand. "Are *you* okay? You seem a little agitated. Is there something wrong?"

"No. I'm fine." She grinned. "Better than fine."

"Anything you want to tell me about?" Esther lowered her voice. "A new guy? Anyone I know?"

Darting glances around the waiting area, Mary nodded, giggled, and blushed. "Yes, but it's a secret."

Esther whispered, "My lips are sealed. Who is it?"

"We have a date this weekend." Shaking her head, the LPN murmured, "He'd kill me if I told you."

Esther shrugged. "Okay, I guess I'll have to wait to find out. Now, who's next?"

****

Yellowstone Ranch Apartment Complex
Billings, Montana

Zena paced the newly built, fully furnished—right down to dishes, pots and pans, linens, and towels—apartment and wondered for the thousandth time if she had made the right decision. It wasn't as if she was *lying* to Jacob. She hadn't mentioned to him that she'd been offered a job with the Montana FBI *before* she agreed to serve on the interagency task force. She hadn't been sure she would like the area or could bear to move away from the east coast—she'd never even been to this part of the country before. The moment she stepped out of the airport and into the Big Sky sunshine, a sense of relief had come upon her. Thousands of miles away from the Adalwolf clan without the sense of their disdain and anger oppressing her every breathing moment, she relished her new-found freedom. Now, as she stood at the window of her stylish apartment and gazed at the mountains in the distance, she knew she had to tell her mother—and Jacob—that she was staying.

What if he thinks I'm doing this to pressure him into more of a relationship?

She had the job offer letter in her phone, proof that this change of employment predated meeting him. But would he believe she wasn't one of *those* women? The desperate, clingy gal who throws herself at a man without thinking about his potential reactions.

163

Screw it. If he didn't like it, too bad. She was her own woman. The Montana FBI was all over the state, even helped out with cases in Wyoming. More likely than not, she'd be moving around the thirteen FBI agencies in Montana, not sitting at the Billings office all the time. Knowing that she might not be assigned here permanently, she'd rented the furnished apartment on a month to month basis. Once she knew where she'd be most of the time, she'd lease a place to live. Right now, much as she loved the Hotel LaBelle, she wouldn't be able to afford staying there, after the assignment was over, even on her new, higher salary.

The doorbell rang and she jumped. "Be right there." She pulled the door open, and her pulse thrummed in her throat. "Thanks for meeting me here, Jacob."

He entered, removed his knit hat, ruffled his hair, and glanced around. "Nice place." He frowned. "Who does it belong to?"

"Me." She closed the door behind him.

The crease in his forehead grew deeper. "You said you're only here for four weeks, that you had to get back to the Indian Country Crimes Unit back in D.C."

"Well, about that." How should she do this? Long or short version? *Tear the band aid off, get it over with.* "The Montana FBI offered me a job before I flew out here. I was on the fence, needed to see if I liked the area before I made this big a move." She shrugged and half-laughed. "I fell in love with Big Sky Country. What can I say? I accepted."

His face grew dark with emotion. "And you're expecting me to do what? Marry you?"

This was *exactly* the reaction she had feared. "No. I

Tears of the Wolf

expect you to say, 'Welcome to Montana, we need a few good men and women.' "

"You know, we were pretty clear at the outset." His lips turned down. "Work together, maybe play together. No complications. I've seen a lot of visitors who come here, say they want to stay. But as soon as things get rough, they leave."

"I can't help what other people do. I've taken the job and committed myself to a three-year contract." She walked to the sliding glass door by the balcony. "We're co-workers who have a lot in common, and we like to flirt with each other." She paused. "We're colleagues, Jacob. Is that so bad?"

"If we're colleagues," he growled, "then why didn't you warn me you were going to arrest my uncle?"

Stunned, she whirled on him. "That's totally inappropriate, and you know it."

His face darkened even more. "If I sent the FBI in to arrest one of your family members, wouldn't you want that professional courtesy—or don't you give a damn about the emotional impact of your actions?"

Incredulous, she stepped away from the window and placed her hands on her hips. "Number one, I am above all a professional. If you needed to take any member of my clan into custody, the last thing you would want to do is to alert a potential accomplice so they could flee. Number two, we all have complicated relationships with our family members—which is why I took you and your mother out of the meeting room, away from the arrest."

"Was the job worth more to you than hurting my mother?"

"Your mother is a tough cookie, Jacob. If you'll recall, she was on board with giving us that mug. If she didn't want to help us, she could have said no."

"She was helping us to find a serial killer—"

"He's a *murderer*." Zena took a deep breath. "Look, I know he's your uncle and you probably have *some* good recollections with him. I'm sure he was like a father figure to you because your dad was gone. Don't the facts outweigh the memories? The man is a sociopath. His whole life is a lie. You saw him murder your father, Jacob. What more do you need to convince you that this is justice—delayed—but still justice?"

"You had no right—"

"I not only had the right, but the duty to follow the leads. If I hadn't followed protocol and done everything by the book, there would have been a federal investigation. Put yourself in my shoes. Would you have told me if the tables were turned?" She paused and lowered her voice. "You're raw. I get it. I'm sorry we didn't have a chance to discuss this right after the arrest. I've been tied up with paperwork—you know what that's like. I'm sorry your uncle murdered your father. I could not have predicted that. The wound of your father's death never healed—and this forced you to relive that night."

"Family matters, but maybe it's different with you. You're so *cold*, so matter of fact about your sisters' deaths. Maybe they didn't mean as much to you as my father and uncle do—did."

Angry tears sprang to her eyes. "When my little sisters were murdered, I was devastated. They were my buddies, my port in the storm of my life as an outcast. I was different, and they protected me. After they were killed, I became the community scapegoat. They called me *Coyote*. Want to know why?"

Lips knife thin, Jacob said nothing as he stared at her, his jaw muscles shuddering with suppressed anger.

"I was *adopted*, a red wolf brought into a pack of gray wolves—because my mother—" she choked out between sobs "—was gunned down in front of me."

He walked a few paces toward the door, then turned back and pulled her into his arms. "I'm sorry. I'm an ass."

"Unlike you, I never forgot a single detail. The hunters chasing us, the shots fired, my mother twisting in the air, howling, then shrieking in pain, the light going out of her eyes as she reverted to her human form." Face on his chest, she sobbed. "I was only a pup. I didn't even know how to turn back into a human. If the Adalwolfs hadn't passed by at that exact moment—"

Her knees buckled and darkness closed in.

****

The moment the angry words flew out of Jacob's mouth he regretted it—and now, with her stretched out on the bed? *I'm a jerk.* He placed his finger on her wrist and her pulse vibrated, slow, but steady. The woman of steel had crumpled under the weight of the memories of her mother's death—and it was all his fault.

If only he had waited another day—or a week. Maybe by then he wouldn't have been so torn up. His mother had remained calm because she didn't want to frighten Eddy. The boy could hear people's thoughts. She had told Jacob neither of them needed to overwhelm him with their emotions. Jacob had avoided the kid as much as he could and took his rage and grief out in night-time runs in his wolf form, scattering rabbits and other small animals with his fierce howls of pain.

Zena stirred and removed the washcloth from her face. "What happened?"

He took the wet rag away. "I was a complete and utter ass and you were—*right*."

She frowned. "What did you say?"

"I'm sorry." He sighed. "You're right. You did everything you should have. Notifying me would have been a major breech in protocol. You had no idea if I would inadvertently signal him that he was a suspect."

She grabbed his large hand with her small one. "Can I get that in writing? I'd like to frame that statement and put it over my desk."

"I'm also sorry about—" he choked up "—your mother. I had no idea."

"It's not a memory I care to share with a lot of people." She squeezed his hand. "I'm sure you don't like telling people about the night your father was murdered."

He shook his head. "Although decades ago, it all came rushing back like it was happening again."

"I know." A tear trickled down the side of her face. "Can I ask you a question?"

He nodded. "Anything."

"Are you mad at me for taking the job?"

He barked out a laugh. "No. I was surprised. Again."

"I'm sorry I took you off guard. It was never my intent to make you feel like I was trying to entrap you. I genuinely love this area. I'm staying."

His lips quirked. "It's not because you can't start

your car?"

"No." She laughed and wiped her face with the back of her hand. "I don't even own a car—yet." She sat up. "Now that we got *that* over with, welcome to my new digs."

"Very nice. Near everything—except me." He stopped. "Did I say that out loud?"

She cocked an eyebrow at him and smirked. "Yes, yes, you did." She shrugged out of her navy-blue blazer. "We could get a little closer, if you'd like."

He took his jacket off and tossed it on the floor. "Did you have a specific distance in mind?"

She reached up and began to unbutton his shirt. "Let's start with six inches—and move on from there."

Slanting his lips against hers, he murmured, "I'd like there to be nothing between us." He slid his hand under her blouse. Her nipples grew hard under his probing fingers, and her breath caught.

"Yes," she breathed, "I agree." She pulled her shirt off and slid out of her bra, offering him perky globes topped by pink areolae and hardened nubs calling to be kissed and sucked.

Arching her back, she moaned, "Too many clothes. We need to get naked."

He stood, breaking the connection, and pulled down her pants, exposing a wispy black thong that barely covered the place he most wanted to be. He ripped them off, and a soft patch of red fluff met his appreciative gaze and touch. He stroked her, running his fingers around her moist nether lips, and delving deep inside her. Zena moaned and rose to meet his probes, her nipples growing harder under his other hand, her wet core clenching his fingers. His pants grew painfully tight, and he paused to yank at his belt.

Face flushed, she sat up, unzipped his jeans, and gasped. "Oh, my. You're a pointer."

"And you're a setter." He grasped her buttocks, lifted her onto his throbbing erection, and she hissed with pleasure.

"You can point that thing at me anytime," she whispered and wrapped her legs around his waist.

"Ever since we met, I've wanted you like this." Bouncing and enjoying her moans, he walked her to a wall and thrust deeper. "And like this."

Zena threw her head back. "Yes. Oh, yes."

He nuzzled her nipples. "Slow and easy? Or hard and fast?"

By way of an answer, she pulled his face up to hers and wrapped her legs tighter around his waist, grinding her pelvis into his. Placing his hands against the wall, he pressed harder, building up the pace and the intensity, not thinking, not remembering, living in the moment, thrusting deeper and harder into this woman who had driven him mad with lust the moment they met. He feared he couldn't hold off another second—

The lady wolf screamed and dug her nails into his back. He plunged deeper, nipped at her neck, and howled.

Chapter Eighteen

Mountain View Park ~*~ Billings, Montana

On a pristine Sunday morning, one week after that annoying woman left his apartment, the Doctor jogged through the undeveloped area of the park he'd found on the Internet. Thanks to the Billings Department of Parks and Recreation, which boasted over two dozen public areas for leisure, he had found this special place. As an added bonus it contained a cemetery. He shivered with anticipation and picked up his pace—his breath coming out in cloudy puffs.

When was the last time he'd been jogging outside, much less in the snow? With his nine to five, Monday through Friday schedule, he'd been forced to join a gym to keep fit. He preferred working out in the morning, before the rest of the world woke up. In those pre-dawn hours, the world was his to conquer. When he entered the doors of the clinic, he might as well have been working in a factory. Line 'em up, bring 'em in, move 'em along. Cattle to be processed, without the pleasure of slaughtering them. *Don't shit where you eat.* Words to live by—and he had. Until now.

Stupid cow. She should have never come to his home. Not that he left his trophies out in full view. *Hardly.* Those rested under a combination in a large velvet-lined jewelry box. Some would call it a safe—

but those people hadn't been safe from him, had they? He snorted at his own joke. The only fly in the ointment, as it were, was that hunk of scalp from his so-called father.

The Doctor hadn't *planned* to tear the old man's skin off. His plan had been to poison the orange geezer and watch him die slowly and in agony—pay back for all the torment he'd been put through in foster care. Instead the bastard died almost the instant he chugged the water and brucine blend. He'd told the old codger it was quinine water, and to expect it to be bitter.

His pain must have been unbearable because the old man accepted the bottle eagerly. Not that he gave a damn about that bum's pain. It was infuriating that he'd died so fast, taking the Doctor's pleasure away—like he'd stolen his childhood. A fit of blind rage had overtaken him, and he'd ripped at the old man's neck with his bare hands—a stupid thing to do. He did the sensible thing and left the heat on high in both the bathroom and the sleeping area to cook the old man until he was too decomposed to reveal any trace DNA evidence.

Done circumnavigating the cemetery, the Doctor slowed his pace. The mausoleum at the top of the hill would be perfect. Once an imposing edifice, the building showed signs of neglect and poor maintenance. The lock took only a little effort to persuade it to open. A lovely workshop. Too bad he hadn't found it for the grocery store clerk. But the burnt building had been close, and he'd been in a hurry. The nights were so cold in this God forsaken place, he'd practically frozen his balls off dragging her out of the car and into the charred ruins. As he recalled that kill and how she died half naked and writhing in pain in his arms, his sweatpants tented. *Ha.* Maybe he'd give Mary what she wanted— and then watch her die, prolonging his exquisite pleasure. Yes, that was *perfect.*

His burner phone buzzed in his pocket, teasing his erection.

"Hi, Mary," he breathed. "You've been on my mind."

"I've been having dreams about you." She lowered her voice. "You are a very naughty boy, and I wake up all hot and bothered. Do you like spanking?"

"It's what the Doctor ordered." He chuckled. "I found a lovely, private spot for us to meet, away from prying eyes and gossiping co-workers. How's five this evening sound to you?"

"Perfect—and come prepared to play. I've been *dying* to see you alone again."

He pressed the end button and laughed. Dying was the key word.

****

Crow Reservation

Esther fed the dog and called to Eddy, "We need to get a move on, or we'll miss the movie."

The boy came bouncing out of his bedroom. "The trailers are almost as good."

"You're right." She checked her bag for car keys. A trip to the ATM was on their agenda for this bright and shiny Sunday, along with shopping for new clothes. *He's growing like a weed.*

Eddy smirked. "I am *not* a weed."

She sighed. "You know you have to watch who you say that stuff to. Not everyone will appreciate it, trust me."

"Don't worry, I know." Hopping in place, he said. "C'mon, Auntie Esther, now *you're* moving slow."

She pulled a flyer out of her purse and handed it to him. "I think you should do this."

"Crow language lessons?" He gave her a dubious look. "What do I need those for?"

"To remember your birthright, your culture, and keep it alive for the next generation." She pulled the door shut behind them and unlocked the car with the remote. "You know the prayers I say at Sabbath dinner?"

"Yeah?" He climbed into the passenger side and buckled his seat belt.

"It's how I pass my Jewish culture along. Hebrew isn't only for prayers—it's the language of Israel. When you know a language, you begin to understand the people—and their history."

"I'm an enrolled member in the Crow Tribe," he protested. "What more do I need?"

She turned to back out of the driveway and paused. "If you want to stay with me, we need to demonstrate that I'm not robbing you of your culture, taking away your collective memories, including the bad ones. We can forgive, but we should never forget the Holocausts—yours and mine."

"Jeez." He sighed and blew his hair out of his eyes. "That's pretty heavy stuff. And a lot of studying. I have a hard enough time with English, much less reading Crow."

She headed to the highway. "That's why I found you a tutor."

"Another teacher?" He slumped down in his seat. "Oh, man."

"I think you might like this one." She flashed him a grin. "She's in high school—won the Miss Crow Nation contest last year."

He put his hands over his face. "You didn't."

"She's cute and poised. I can see why she won. She wants to be a nurse, so she volunteers at the clinic."

He peeked through his fingers. "I'll be picked on at school—again."

Esther shook her head. "Tutoring will be done at home, and she's been asked to keep it confidential."

"In other words, I don't have a choice."

"See, you understand me completely." She pressed down on the gas pedal. "The show starts at five. As long as you don't dawdle, we'll have enough time to buy you some new pants, a couple of long sleeve shirts, a sweater or two, a good winter coat, and some new boots."

"Cowboy?"

She rolled her eyes. "Are there any other kind?"

He grinned. "Okay, I'll try to learn Crow. My mother and grandmother would probably like me to."

Esther smiled. *Yes, they will*.

Eddy's mouth gaped, and his eyes widened. "They will? As in they're still around?"

"Like my husband, they are always with us. Don't ever forget that."

"Have you—" His voice dropped to a whisper. "—seen them?"

"I didn't want to scare you, honey." She patted his hand. "They never left you. They've been at your side every day."

"Miss Zena told me that if I asked them to show me a sign that they were around, they would answer me."

"And?"

He dug into his jacket pocket. "Look at this." He opened his fist revealing a handful of colorful beads. "I've been finding these everywhere I go." Wide-eyed, he whispered, "They heard me."

"Yes, they did. And they are awfully proud of you."

The rest of the ride was spent in silence. She knew it was a lot for the boy to take in, but she also knew he could do it. Like her, he came from strong stock. He would grow up to be a good man—perhaps even a great man—one who was in touch with his family and his heritage.

****

Mountain View Park ~*~ Billings, Montana

The Doctor stood in the doorway of the mausoleum and watched Mary Longbow slog her way up the hill. *The woman is seriously out of shape.* As he watched her struggle, his nascent interest in having sex with her began to droop. He wondered why she carried a backpack, then shook off the idea. *Who cares? She's mine to do with as I want.*

"Hey there," he called. "You okay? You need help?"

Puffing, she shook her head. "I'm. Fine."

Sure, you are. Stepping back into the dank space, he threw a log on the fire he'd built in an alcove. A blanket and pillow lay across a stone casket, one of three in the room, setting the stage for the drama soon to unfold. The stupid cow had been begging for a kinky sex adventure ever since she'd arrived without warning at his apartment. She'd cornered him repeatedly at work, and he'd warned her off with frowns and head shakes. But she'd been frigging relentless. *Be careful what you wish for, my dear.*

"Whew, there you are." Mary entered the building, glanced around the space, and grinned. "So romantic, you even built a fire. Where are my flowers?"

He placed his hand on his chest. "You're the only flower we need in here."

"Ha." She slipped the backpack off. "I bet you say that to all the girls."

He stepped past her and closed the door. "No need to let the cold breeze in."

"Kinky, private, and cheap." She put a finger up. "Give me a moment to catch my breath."

He closed the gap between them and pulled her knit hat off. Her long black hair tumbled down her back, and the urge to stroke it was irresistible. "You have lovely hair."

"Thanks to my full-blooded Cheyenne mother. She had the best hair in the tribe, never turned gray." She removed her down coat and placed it on top of a concrete casket along with her backpack. "Nice and cozy in here."

"We'll be hot and bothered soon." He chuckled at his own words, and at the thought of the brucine-filled syringe under the pillow. Once he had her naked and bound, she'd be totally at his mercy. He couldn't *wait* to hold her in his arms as she writhed in her death throes.

Mary pulled a white packet out of the pocket of her scrubs and tapped its contents into the water bottle. "Cold air gives me sinus headaches."

Apprehension seized him. It couldn't be—could it?

Sharon Buchbinder

It looked like the plain over the counter remedy he liked to alter with brucine. "What are you taking?"

"Something Esther gave me. She said she got it from you." Mary lifted the bottle to her lips.

"No," he shouted. "Don't drink it." He lunged for the bottle.

Shaking her head and rolling her eyes, she chugged the entire bottle before falling to the floor in convulsions.

"You stupid bitch," he screamed, his voice echoing off the stone walls. "You've ruined everything."

****

Yellowstone Ranch Apartment Complex ~*~
Billings, Montana

Zena rolled over in bed and smiled. She tiptoed her fingers down Jacob's chest to his hips, and then his rock-hard erection. She chuckled. "I'm happy to see you, too."

He rolled over on top of her and held her wrists over her head with one hand. "You dare to awake the beast?"

Wriggling beneath him, she laughed. "The fiend was up long before I was."

"Don't move," he warned. "I have nefarious plans for you, ones that will make you walk like a bowlegged cowboy."

Zena bucked. "You going to do something, or are you going to talk me to death?"

"As a matter of fact, I have divided your topography into sections." He kissed her neck. "I plan to start here." He moved downward, nibbling and kissing. "Then I will move to the twin peaks." He sucked and pulled at her nipples, giving each its due.

178

"When I finish with those, I will wander south." Trailing kisses, he paused at her belly button. "I will explore this intriguing cave." Jacob's tongue worked into her innie.

"You're tickling me," she giggled. "Kind of ruins the mood."

He quirked an eyebrow. "I'm an intrepid explorer, a scout looking for sweet grazing—which I see at the fork of the two birch trees." He plunged his tongue deep into her core, savoring her salty flavor, licking everywhere except her excited bundle of nerves.

"Ohmigod. You are *such* a tease."

He looked up and mock frowned. "Quiet. I have much more exploring to do before I spark your tinder."

Between gasps of pleasure she laughed. "You're really into playing Indian scout. There's a shocker. Why doesn't that surprise me even a little bit?"

He paused and ran his fingers around her wet lips. "You want me to play with you some more?"

"No—yes—omigod, omigod, you have got to—"

Sliding his erection into her molten center, he stopped moving. She writhed and screamed in frustration, vainly attempting to grab his hair. "Yes, let it all out. You've been much too tense."

She wrapped her legs over his back and rose to meet him repeatedly until, at last he could hold back no more. With a final thrust, he howled and collapsed on top of her, panting. "You killed the scout. He can go no farther."

She burst into raucous laughter and pulled him in for a kiss. "Next time, I'm the explorer."

On the nightstand, their phones buzzed and danced. He glanced at the phones and then at Zena—her face mirroring his emotions—anxiety and dread. A call during nighttime seldom held any good news. He sighed, rolled off his lovely pixie, and grabbed his cell—but the phone stopped vibrating. The caller ID said Yellowstone County Police.

Zena now held her cell phone to her ear. "Be there as soon as I can."

"Is it—"

She nodded and her eyes filled with tears. "You need to call Tommy Otterlegs. He has some bad news."

He tapped the smart phone and his friend's sad voice came through the line. "Thanks for calling me back, Jacob." Tommy paused. "It's another woman—" His voice faltered. "She's cut up pretty bad. Can't ID her—yet."

Puzzled, Jacob asked, "Is Joe there?"

Tommy gulped and his voice shook. "Yeah, he's here. He wanted me to call you, since we're relatives. Said it would be better coming from a family member."

Jacob jumped to his feet and shouted, "What the hell? Spit it out."

His cousin's voice grew hoarse. "She's wearing blue scrubs. We think it might be Aunt Esther."

His fingers went numb, and the phone slipped from his hand. He stared at Zena, unseeing, and tears rolled down his face. He screamed, "Not my mother, no, not my mother, no, no, no—"

Warm arms wrapped around his waist and soft, soothing words rolled over him. "They don't know, Jacob. It might be someone else—some other poor woman." She squeezed him harder. "Whatever happens, I'm here for you."

Chapter Nineteen

Mountain View Park ~*~ Billings, Montana

Fear gripped his heart as Jacob and Zena rode into the cemetery portion of the city park. Zena had insisted on driving. At first he'd argued, but then finally he'd seen the sense in her words. He'd blacked out the night his father had been murdered. He didn't want to chance hurting someone by going into a fugue state or having a PTSD panic attack. Repeated calls to his mother's cell phone went to voice mail. She didn't respond to texts, either. Where had she gone? Why wasn't she answering him? Hitting the end button on his phone yet another time, he sat silent in the passenger seat. As the GPS told them the way to the crime scene, he hoped against hope that it was a case of mistaken identity.

The headlights bounced up and down in front of the vehicle, revealing snow-dusted headstones marching across the hills. *So many dead people.* He prayed, begging God. *Please, don't let it be my mother.*

The robotic woman's voice announced, "You have arrived at your destination."

Zena unbuckled, leaned over, and kissed him. "I'm with you, no matter what."

Numb with shock and dread, he climbed out of the car. A circle of brilliant lights turned night into day, illuminating the crowd of uniforms awaiting him.

Yellow tape flapped, and the night wind howled across the hill like a wolf crying for its mate. A large mausoleum hulked in the center of a circle of pine trees, the name of a prominent Billings family chiseled over the door. He paused, looking around for Tommy's face, but not seeing him.

"I'm here." His cousin waved from the entrance and pointed into the void. "The CSI team's in here, working the scene." He pointed at the coroner's wagon. "Joe's waiting for you over there."

"Who found her?"

"A bloodhound." Tommy shook his head. "The owners were training him for wilderness search and rescue. Apparently, they had planted some items for him to find, but when they let him off the leash, he made a beeline for this place. By the time they caught up to him, he was frantic, digging at the door, wouldn't stop howling. The trainer took one look and called 9-1-1."

Jacob tried to push his way in, but his bantam rooster relative shoved him back.

Tommy pulled the heavy metal door behind him, leaving a sliver of bright light leaking around the edges. "First of all, you don't want to see this. Second of all, if you screw up my crime scene, I'm going to be unhappy."

"I need to see, Tommy." Jacob stood more than a head taller than his cousin. If he could get the entry open, all he had to do was stand in front of him and look over his head. He reached past Tommy and tried to push at the door. "I need to know—"

"Dammit, I said no." The little guy placed his hands on Jacob's chest and shoved him so hard, he slammed back into Zena.

"Come with me, Jacob," she said in a low voice.

He balled his hands into fists and glared at his cousin. "Your mother died in a hospital, surrounded by people trying to save her. My mother died alone here in this—this—tribute to death. You have to let me see where she died."

Zena plucked at his arm. "You don't even know for sure that it's her. Come on. Let's find Joe."

"I will not abandon my mother. I will not hide like I did the night my father was murdered. I want to see how she died." Tears sprang to his eyes. "I don't give a damn if you think I'm being irrational. There's nothing rational about love *or* murder."

Pursing his lips, Tommy shook his head but stepped away from the entrance. "You can look, but don't go in."

A CSI tech in a hazmat suit, goggles, and booties paused in his recitation of evidence to a team member as Jacob stepped onto the marble threshold—and stopped. *Blood.* All he could see was blood. The walls, the floor, everywhere he looked inside the monument was coated with crimson edged with brown—and reeked of death. A sound like a primal scream rose from his throat and echoed through the hills in the night. In the distance, coyotes howled back.

Tugging at his arm, Zena murmured, "You've seen enough."

He allowed her to propel him through the snow-covered grass to the county vehicle. Joe jumped out of the front seat and nodded at Jacob. "I'm sorry for your loss. We needed you to ID her—she's been—" he paused "—her face is—" voice thick, he choked on the word "—mutilated."

Jacob had been a cop a long time and he believed nothing could shock him anymore but was wrong. The idea of his mother's beautiful face, her bright, intelligent eyes, warm and compassionate, being maimed made his stomach roil. He took a deep breath and swallowed hard to keep the bile down. His voice came out in a hoarse whisper. "Show me."

Opening the back doors of the black van, Joe climbed inside and invited Jacob and Zena to come in with him. "Brace yourself."

Joe unzipped the black body bag halfway down, stopping at the woman's waist, which was twisted in an unnatural position.

"Jesus," Zena breathed and gripped his hand. "The work of a monster."

Her face and hair were *gone*—and all that remained were eyeballs and muscle—and even that was sliced up.

Black spots began to dance in his vision, and he gripped the side of the gurney, bowing his head. Something caught his eye, something out of place on the woman's shoulder.

A feather tattoo.

"It's not my mother," he breathed, almost fainting with relief—but still sickened by the sight before him. "She doesn't have any tattoos."

A long moment of silence passed as Jacob took it all in. *Not my mother. Not my mother. Ohmigod, thank God, it's not my mother.*

Breaking the silence at last, Zena whispered, "She looks like a contortionist frozen in place. It has to be the same guy. He's gone berserk."

As Jacob leaned against the inside of the van to steady his rubbery legs, his phone buzzed and vibrated in his pocket. Hands shaking, he yanked the mobile out, only to drop it on the floor of the vehicle. Tears pricked his eyes as he retrieved and read the caller ID. It was his mother. She was safe.

As he put the phone to his ear, the questions ran through his mind like a broken record.

Who is this woman? And who will the bastard kill next?

****

Yellowstone County Medical Examiner and Coroner's Office
Billings, Montana

"Thanks for meeting us here, Mrs. Graywolf," Joe Hager said after he introduced himself. "Your son talks about you a lot."

"All good, I hope." Esther chuckled. "You never know with kids."

Jacob shook his head. "Mom, I always tell everyone how great you are."

"What can I do for you?" When she'd spoken to her son an hour ago, he'd been so anxious to know she was okay, he'd made her nervous. "You didn't tell me on the phone, so I'm in the dark."

Zena bent down and said, "Eddy, why don't you and I go find the vending machine?"

Glancing between the adults, the boy motioned for Esther to bend down. He whispered in her ear, "Someone's dead." His voice grew rough. "They were afraid it was you."

Sighing, she knelt down and hugged the kid who had wormed his way into her heart. "Thank you, honey.

I'll be okay. You go with Zena. You can have anything you want." She stood and he gave her a questioning look. "What's one more piece of junk food after all the soda, popcorn, and candy we ate at the movies?

Zena put a hand on his shoulder and pointed him toward the exit. "What's your favorite candy bar?"

After the door swung shut, she turned to Jacob. "Well?"

"The body of a woman was found today." he paused, as if searching for the right words. "She was wearing blue scrubs that had the Indian Health Services laundry label on them."

Her breath caught in her throat. "What do you need me to do?"

"Mom," Jacob said, "I want you to sit down."

Joe scooted a rolling chair behind her, and she sat. Ordinarily not a handwringer, she began to twist her gloves.

"Was it one of my co-workers?"

"Perhaps." Jacob passed his hand over his face. "There was nothing to identify her at the crime scene. No purse, no wallet, not even a scrap of paper."

The clinic team was almost like a family. A death in the group would hit everyone hard, much less a murder. "Can't you take a picture of her face, run it against the employee ID photos?"

His lips thinned, and he squeezed his eyes shut. "She has no face."

"I don't understand." She loved her son, but he was making no sense. "How could she not have a face?'"

Joe cleared his throat. "Her body was disfigured, and she was, for lack of a better word—scalped."

The room whirled, and her gorge rose in her throat.

She put her face in her hands and took deep gulps of cool air. Thank God she was sitting down. Attempting to compose herself, Esther spoke between her fingers. "We all need criminal background checks to work there. You can get her fingerprints."

A gentle hand rested on her shoulder. Jacob spoke softly, "Burned off—after she was dead."

"Small mercies," she murmured, horrified at the tortures this woman suffered.

"We've asked for the DNA to be run. If she's not in those databases, we won't be able to ID her. Which is why we need your help."

"Anything."

"Do any of your women co-workers have a feather tattoo on their shoulder?"

She shook her head—then stopped at the memory of her friend's excitement at her new body art for earning her LPN. "Wait—omigod, no. It *can't* be Mary Longbow—I saw her on Friday."

Tears poured between her fingers, and she sobbed uncontrollably. Esther and Mary hadn't been best friends, but they'd liked each other, worked well together, laughed at the same things. No one deserved this type of death.

"You need some water?" Jacob asked.

Esther shook her head. "Poor Mary. She got her life together—even had a new boyfriend."

Jacob patted her arm. "You're doing great. Any idea who the guy is?"

"She wouldn't tell me—but I'm pretty sure it's someone who works with us. Mary said he'd kill her if anyone found out."

"That doesn't sound good. We're going to come

with you to the clinic tomorrow, ask a few questions." He paused. "Not a word to anyone, Mom, okay?"

"Of course not, but ohmigod, Jacob." She grabbed his hand. A dreadful idea lay in her stomach like a ball of lead, ready to explode. "The killer could be someone I know—someone I work with every day." Her skin crawled as if an army of ants marched over her. "These murders only started this summer, that we know of, right?"

"One was in early June, but yes, it was in the summer."

"That's when the new doctors arrived." And she wasn't sure which one was more concerning—the arrogant and demanding blond, or the dark-haired Teddy Bear with the baleful demeanor. Either way, there would be a serial killer in the next exam room when she returned to work.

Chapter Twenty

Crow Indian Health Services ~*~ Crow Agency

The Doctor slammed the apartment door shut and didn't give a shit who heard him. "Stupid bitch," he snarled under his breath. Why did she have to go and suck all the joy out of his life? He had waited all week, perfected his plan, created the ideal kill room—in a cemetery. The irony of it had appealed to him on so many levels—but she had the last laugh, destroying his hard-earned pleasures, ruining it for him. *However, I got the last laugh.*

Standing in the glass enclosed shower, he shampooed the bloody mass of hair—his token. he took care in applying a new conditioner the wig company assured him would keep the driest hair in pristine, shining condition. He might have gone a bit overboard with her face and fingertips, but he had no choice. There was nothing to be done about it now. It was the stupid cow's own fault. She broke his cardinal rule. *Don't shit where you eat.*

Satisfied with his efforts, he climbed out of the shower and pinned the scalp to a Styrofoam head. He combed the luxuriant locks out to dry, taking care not to pull too hard. These treasures required a gentle touch. With a bit of luck, this could be his best one. Not to say he was about to stop. He chuckled. *I'm still behind Dr.*

Death. If only he could have met the Brit, shook his hand, and learned his dark arts. Alas, Dr. Death was unreachable. He was, in fact, dead. *Suicide. Such a pity.* He would have made a brilliant mentor.

The Doctor removed the brilliant blue contact lenses he wore to cover the one thing that betrayed any hint of his heritage, his light brown eyes. Combing his blond hair, he mused at how he looked so *white,* yet was almost half Native American. Not that he planned to try to enroll in a tribe anytime in the near future. He grinned at himself in the mirror. Now that *would* be a happy hunting ground. Funny how genetics worked. The photo showed his father as a handsome young man, with hair that was almost white. Not as good-looking as him, of course, but sort of like a fun house mirror image of himself. Northern German genes, according to the genealogy report tucked in the old man's suitcase at that disgusting motel room. He'd disposed of everything else that identified his father, of course, by tossing them into the deepest part of the Yellowstone River he could find. The same way he'd ditched that dumb bitch's backpack.

He chuckled. A mask, a corset, a whip—she had expected to have a good time at his expense. Boy was she surprised. Admiring his charismatic smile, he wondered who he could entice next. While he didn't like to shit where he ate, he had to admit, there had been a certain frisson of anticipation every time he saw Mary at the clinic. Who would be next? She had to have beautiful long black hair. That was a given. And she'd have to be smart, maybe even sassy, to make the thrill of the kill more intense. Maybe someone prominent in the community to show no one was safe from him. The news would be full of him and his prowess—and how unsolvable the case was. Talk about an added adrenaline rush.

He climbed into bed and turned the nightstand lamp off. A light in his head went on. The woman was a pain in the ass, but she fit the bill in every other way. Long black hair, arrogant, condescending. He'd show her who was boss. *How should I do it?* In reviewing each kill, he considered what he'd done wrong with each of them—and what he'd done right. This one was so close to home, the fantasy of brushing past her, accidentally bumping into her, all the while knowing she was next, left him breathless and aroused. What if she sensed his eagerness? Would she get anxious? Try to avoid him? Run into the break room to get away from him? Like a kid at Christmas, he could not stop fantasizing about her and what he was going to do to her. He was so excited he wasn't sure he could get to sleep. A new hunt would begin tomorrow, and he could hardly wait.

****

Crow Reservation ~~ Billings, Montana*

A wave of nostalgia swept over Esther as Eddy stumbled into the kitchen scratching his head. The kid looked and acted so much like her son at that age.

"Morning, sleepyhead. Oatmeal's ready."

"With raisins and brown sugar?" He yawned. Jessie chuffed and placed her head in Eddy's lap for an ear scratching.

"Of course. Is there any other way to serve it?"

He pulled up a chair. "If you run out of raisins and brown sugar, all you have is a pot of glue."

She placed the steaming bowl in front of him along

with a mug of hot cocoa. "If that's all you have to eat, it's better than nothing."

"Aunt Esther, have you ever been hungry? Like your stomach growling so hard, you wondered if you'd ever eat again?"

Such a serious question at this hour of the morning deserved a careful response. "I have not. But I know there are those who are—many are our neighbors." In fact, she had a list of items she had promised to pick up for the elder food pantry. While not a regular volunteer, she gave money and shopped for the director when they needed specific items from Billings. "Why do you ask?"

"One of my classmates never has lunch. He goes to the library while we eat."

"That's awful." She dared not say what she truly wanted to say—but then again, he'd only read her mind. Time to clean up her mental language. "Isn't he eligible for the free lunch program?"

Shoveling a spoon of cereal into his mouth, Eddy shook his head. "Something about his parents making too much money? I don't understand it all."

Esther didn't understand it either. Almost half the families had kids on free or reduced lunch. Why wouldn't someone cough up a few bucks to cover his? Lunch shaming was such a shitty thing to do.

"I heard that." He pointed at a newly created swear jar sitting next to the stove. "Put a quarter in."

"Later. I have a lot of bad words for this. I'll put in five bucks. What do you want to do about your classmate's situation?"

His voice hesitant, he asked, "Would it be okay if I took two lunches to school every day and gave one to him?"

Esther's heart was so full, she thought it would burst. After all this little guy had been through, he had such a kind soul. Tears stung her eyes. "I think that's a wonderful idea. We can start today."

He jumped up and ran around the table to give her a hug. "Thank you. It will be our *mitzvah*."

Brushing her cheeks, she laughed. "Who taught you that word—and how to use it?"

"I did," Jacob said. He strolled into the kitchen and scooped oatmeal from the pot into a crockery bowl. "We talked about how it means good deeds."

"When did you get in? And where's Zena?"

He threw her a sharp look. "Three in the morning and she's at her new apartment."

"Oh, of course, silly me." Esther winked at her son. "I'm glad you're here. Could you please take Eddy to school for me? I need to run to Billings."

Jacob stared at her. "What about our plans this morning?"

"I forgot I had taken the morning off to get supplies for the elder food pantry. They're running low on a lot of things. I can't let them down." She hoped he didn't ask any more questions. With Eddy around, it was difficult to keep a secret.

"Who has a secret?" Eddy piped up.

She gave him the look. "Everyone has secrets, my friend. And you don't need to go blabbing them around. Got it?"

Chastened, he nodded. "Yes, ma'am."

"Go get ready for school while I pack an extra lunch for you." Esther waved him toward his room. "Time's a wasting."

Jacob placed a hip against the stove and sipped his coffee. "What's going on?"

She sighed. So much for keeping secrets. "I do have to get food for the pantry. But I have another errand I need to run that involves our new doctors."

"Spill it."

"I have a friend who's an administrator with Indian Health Services Physician Credentialing. I want to ask her in person to do some digging into the doctors' backgrounds. I have a hunch—woman's intuition, shall we say?"

Jacob quirked a brow at her. "Zena and I should be doing that, not you."

"You don't go back thirty years with this person. She won't tell you a thing without a subpoena. How long would that take, and which judge do you want to annoy today?"

Shaking his head, he set the cup down. "You find out anything, you call me immediately. Am I clear?"

She nodded. "Crystal. See you at the clinic this afternoon." She glanced at her watch and yelled, "Eddy, time to go! Jacob doesn't have all day to wait for you."

****

Crow Indian Health Services ~*~ Crow Agency

The Doctor strolled in the front door at his usual time, ten after nine, right after someone else made the first pot of coffee in the morning. His normal routine was to enter the break room, act surprised the brewing was already in process, and then grab the first cup for himself. Today there'd be a slight change. After getting his coffee, he planned to meander out to the reception desk and stake out a good perch to be on the lookout for his prey. When he arrived, however, the place was almost empty, except for the security guard at the front door. He asked the man where everyone was and noticed his face matched the color of his gray uniform.

Feigning concern the Doctor asked, "What's wrong? You look terrible."

Tears glittered in the guard's eyes. "Death in the family."

"Immediate family?"

"My cousin, Mary Longbow."

Despite his attempt at not showing emotion, the Doctor gasped, and his heart jerked erratically. *Shit. Shit. Shit.* That mausoleum door had been shut. How had they found her so soon? With the snow and the remote location, she should have been hidden for weeks, if not months. He needed to hit something but balled his hands into a fist and bowed his head, murmuring through gritted teeth, "So sorry for your loss."

"The administrator wants all the employees in the break room for a meeting at one o'clock." The guard shook his head and sighed. "She was happy as a lark on Friday, looking forward to the weekend. Hard to believe she's gone."

The Doctor's mind whirled. What would a co-worker do and say in this situation? He tried to look sad and compassionate, two alien ideas, and hoped he pulled it off. "She will be missed."

The other man choked up and croaked out, "Thank you."

Stunned and confused, the Doctor found his way to the break room where people stood in clusters, whispering.

"So sad."

"She just got her LPN license."

"What a shame."

"Always so cheerful."

His head was about to explode with annoyance, and he bit his tongue to keep from screaming, *She's no saint. She wanted to tie me up and flog me—do kinky shit.* He took a deep breath and let it out. *Calm down, before you blow everything.* He made his way to the coffee pot. It was empty. These selfish pricks had not left him a single drop. He'd have to make a new pot, one of his most despised work tasks. Banging the cupboard open, he pulled out a filter, filled it with ground coffee, and yanked the carafe out of the machine. It slammed into the faucet and shattered, scattering glass shards everywhere. The quiet conversations ceased, and everyone stared at him— some with expressions of surprise, others glaring at him with open disapproval.

Shit. Shit. Shit. Could this day get any worse?

The administrator appeared in the break room doorway and glanced around, her gaze coming to a rest on him. She nodded and crooked a finger. "Doctor, could I have a minute with you, please?"

"Sure." A nervous tic made his eyelid jump, and his voice sounded hoarse to his own ears. "Let me clean this mess up and I'll be right there." He attempted a chuckle. "I sure hope there's an extra pot that fits this machine, otherwise, I'll have to run out to the store and get one."

"Lou, could you grab the broom, please. There's a spare pot in the cabinet over the refrigerator. Have someone tall get it down." She held the door open. "Now that's taken care of," she nodded at the Doctor, "we can have our conversation—in my office."

"Be right there." He tossed the handle into the trashcan and followed her out to a hum of curious voices.

The administrator gestured toward her space, pointed to a seat, and closed the door. "I'm sure you're wondering why I've asked you to meet with me." She turned the computer monitor around to face the Doctor. On the screen was a photo of the orange-tinged old geezer. "Could you please tell me who this man is and why you needed to meet with him in my office?"

Chapter Twenty-One

Crow Indian Health Services Parking Lot ~*~ Crow Agency

"My friend asked to remain anonymous. Push comes to shove, she said you can subpoena her, and she'll be willing to testify in court." Esther pulled out a folder and handed several documents to Zena and Jacob. "By way of giving you some context, all doctors in the US are followed from the moment they graduate from medical school until the day they die. They're considered national resources—plus if they screw up, they can hurt a lot of people. So, they have to be tracked."

As she reviewed one document Zena murmured, "Job hopper—and gaps on this resume."

"High mobility physicians are typically identified and not hired by Indian Health Services." Esther tapped the resume Zena held. "Big red flags. Frequent job changes often indicate problems with getting along with people. Missing time is also troubling. Physicians don't usually drop out to 'find themselves'. Both raise questions about drug use, mental illness—or worse."

"This other guy has only been in two jobs—his residency training site and Indian Health Services."

"Employers want a predictable physician—not the erratic trouble-maker."

Jacob looked up from the papers. "Even so, there's nothing criminal here."

She sighed. "What's not on that resume are sexual harassment charges, inappropriate comments to patients, disciplinary files that were destroyed—all swept under the rug because the previous employers didn't want bad publicity."

"I don't understand," Zena said. "If your friend had all that information at her fingertips, why did Indian Health Services let him come here?"

"The previous administrator overruled the usual safeguards." She shook her head. "He had a new job, was leaving in June, and only needed someone with a pulse."

Zena's phone buzzed. "Joe texted me a book. Give me a minute." She waved her hand. "Talk amongst yourselves."

Jacob crumpled the paper. "Thanks to him, we have a killer in our midst."

"Yes," Esther agreed. "Lives lost, families destroyed, all because one person decided the rules didn't matter."

Jacob shook his head. "So many lives."

"I vote for him," Esther said tapping a resume. "He's been more than a little off from the day he walked in the door."

"Guys, guys," Zena yelled, her words tumbling out in a rush. "We've got him!" She held her phone up. "The DNA from Mr. Doe, the FBI ran it through a genealogical database and got two hits. The orange guy and—" her face flushed "—a first degree relative."

"Speak slowly for the cheap seats." Jacob placed a hand on her arm. "Take a breath."

"He killed his father." Zena snatched the resumé out of Esther's hand. "This guy—and I'm betting all those women, too. We have probable cause."

"Hold on," Jacob said. "Just because he's related to John Doe doesn't make him the killer."

"Seriously?" She quirked an eyebrow at him. "The killer used his bare hands to rip the skin off his father's neck. He left his DNA in the wound—and expected the heat to destroy any evidence. We have probable cause to make an arrest. Let's do this."

"Hold on," Jacob said. "We can't go in there like a SWAT team. There are patients and employees in there. We need to isolate him."

"Good idea," Zena agreed and released the door handle. "You want me to call for back up?"

"Yes and no." He sighed. "My tribe has seen enough of the FBI in full force for a while. There are still members complaining about how Redhawk's arrest was handled."

"We did it by the book," Zena protested. "There was no brutality. We had hundreds of people in that room. Not a single person was hurt."

"I hear you, but perceptions are real. I'm trying to prevent another scene and stirring up bad feelings in the community."

Zena folded her arms across her chest. "What do you propose?"

"Mom, I want you to go in there and act like it's a regular day at work. Can you do that?"

"Yes. That's all?"

"No." Jacob shook his head. "Call me with an update on this guy's whereabouts. If he didn't show up for work, then we need to go looking for him. If he's in there, I need you to put me on his schedule as a patient."

Esther laughed. "That's never going to work. He'll see you coming and take off." She eyed Zena. "Has he ever met you?"

"Not that I can recall." She quirked an eyebrow. "Always a first time. How's this for a cover story—I have intense migraines and nothing I've taken before works."

"Perfect," Esther nodded. "The good news is, I doubt he'll want to take a biopsy of your scalp—thanks to your red hair."

"Okay," Jacob interrupted. "Call us when you have an appointment time. I'm going to see if Bronco is around."

Zena's brow furrowed. "What do we need a remote viewer for?"

"In addition to being a biker looking dude with huge biceps, Bronco's a former Special Agent with the Alcohol, Tobacco, and Firearms Agency." He grinned. "He and his wife, Emma, took down a Nazi hate group and human trafficking operation, almost single-handedly. Since he's not entitled to use Indian Health Services, he's hasn't encountered our unsub—and he lives on the rez. People trust him. They won't freak out if they see him in the clinic."

"Well, shoot," Zena muttered. "Why didn't you tell me he's your secret weapon?"

"You're the secret weapon." Esther tapped Zena's hand. "Keep your hoodie pulled down and wear sunglasses so the patients in the waiting room don't recognize you."

"Put your earpiece in. When we're in place, I'll

give you a signal and you can make the collar." Jacob growled. "Let's get this bastard."

****

Indignant, the Doctor placed his hand on his chest and spat at the administrator, "You've been *spying* on me? There are privacy laws, you know."

"When you were hired, you were advised that this federal installation has video monitoring in all areas except exam rooms and rest rooms." The administrator pulled out a document and showed it to him. "That's your signature, isn't it?"

"Yes, but I've been asking for a private office ever since I got here," the Doctor protested. "If I had one, I wouldn't have been forced to use yours. This is all *your* fault."

"Seriously?" Disbelief filled the administrator's voice.

"How many times do I have to tell you? He didn't belong here." The Doctor's eye twitched, annoying him. "I met with him to humor him, then I sent him to St. Vic's. He's an addict looking for pain meds."

"An addict?" The administrator twisted the computer monitor around and hit the play button on a video. "Funny. He gave you something—not the other way around. A photo. You look pretty upset."

Heart in his throat, the Doctor watched his life unravel on the screen before him. *Think, man, think. A lie with a nugget of truth. That works.* He exhaled a long sigh and put a sad expression on his face.

The bitch stared at him—her lips tight.

"Okay, okay." He put his hands up in surrender. "You got me. He's a relative—my uncle."

She waited for three beats. "And?"

"I was upset because—" he choked up, surprising himself with his authenticity "—he came to tell me my sister was dead." He put his face in his hands. "My parents are dead, now my sister. It was very distressing."

"Which is why you tossed him out?" She inclined her head toward at the video where the Doctor gesticulated at the old man and pointed at the door. "You were distraught?"

"Yes, yes." His eyes welled with tears. "I wasn't thinking straight."

"We all respond to death in different ways. Seems yours is anger." She paused. "Have you reached out and made up with him?"

He nodded. "That's all behind us now."

"All families have their ups and downs. I'm sorry for your loss."

"Thank you." The urge to laugh crept up his throat, and he tamped it down. "So, I can use your office?"

"Absolutely not. Find another place for your family reunions." She gave him a hard look. "I'm writing a note to your file, including your extenuating circumstances. One more incident, however, and I will be forced to take disciplinary measures. Got it?"

He nodded. "I understand." What was he supposed to say now? *Oh, that's right.* "I'm sorry. I never meant to violate your trust. I won't ever do it again."

"Good." She stood. "I have to prepare for a meeting. You can return to work now."

"Of course." He gave a little bow. "Your wish is my command."

One of these days, that bitch will get what she has coming. But not today. Right now, I have better prey to find.

As he left the administrator's office, the scheduling clerk called to him. "Doctor, you have an urgent add-on. She's in exam room three. We left the lights off because she's having a terrible migraine. I told her those were your specialty."

"Yes, they are." He smiled in anticipation of long black hair. *Today is going to be a good day, after all.* He rapped at the door, walked in, and said, "Ms. Adalwolf?"

A tiny woman perched on the edge of a chair, her toes barely touching the floor. Hoodie pulled over her face, sunglasses covering her eyes, she whispered, "Yes, that's me."

He took a seat across from her on a rolling stool and pulled up the electronic health record. *Odd. She wasn't in there. Maybe because they squeezed her in?* "How long have you been having these headaches?"

Placing her hands on her temples, she murmured, "Since I was a teenager, when I got my first period."

"On a scale of one to ten, where one is no pain and ten is excruciating, how would you describe your headache right now."

"Eleven."

"What medications have you taken in the past for these migraines? Acetaminophen, aspirin, caffeine, a mix of those three?"

"Yes."

"Ibuprofen, naproxen, any of the triptans?"

"Yes, and I've done biofeedback."

"I'll need to do an examination." His fingers tingled at the prospect of running them through her long black hair. "Could you please remove your head covering?"

She flipped back her hoodie and flaming red hair tumbled down her back. He bit back a gasp. *I did not see that coming.* "Unusual to see a ginger around here."

"Irish father, Native mother."

He palpated her temples and the base of her scalp, inquiring where the pain was the worst, avoiding her wireless earbuds. *Don't these people ever take them out of their ears?*

"In my eyeballs," she moaned and pressed her lids tight. "My right eye feels like someone stuck an ice pick in it."

"Can I take a look?"

She nodded and removed her sunglasses. Beautiful green eyes looked up at him, and he examined them with an ophthalmoscope. "No irregularities."

"It hurts so much," she whined. "Don't you have *anything* for the pain?"

"Hmm." *Drug seeking behavior, a real addict.* His lips twisted with disgust, and his fingers itched with the desire to pull the syringe out of his pocket and plunge it into her neck to shut her up. He didn't ordinarily like redheads, but he might have to make an exception in this case. Her hair was exceptionally soft and silky. *Don't shit where you eat.* Maybe she'd be willing to meet him somewhere else, like the others had. Buying time as he weighed his options, he glanced at her paperwork. A student at the local community college, she was studying criminology. He laughed at the irony. "So, you want to be a cop?"

"FBI."

"Don't they have height requirements? You're a little too small for that, aren't you?"

She gave him an inexplicable smile and nodded. "You know, I've heard that all my life. Funny thing—I'm big enough to carry this." Flashing an ID card, she announced, "FBI. Doctor Brett Turner, you are under arrest for the murder of Alfred Guenter Turner—your father."

The door swung open and Jacob Graywolf rushed in, followed by a giant of a man in a black leather jacket. Panic rose in his chest and he looked around the tiny space for an exit. Trapped like a wild animal—he had no choice.

He leaped at the woman and whirled her in front of him like a human shield. Holding the syringe inches from her neck, he snarled, "One wrong move and this bitch dies."

Chapter Twenty-Two

Crow Indian Health Services Parking Lot ~*~
Crow Agency

Zena climbed into the driver's seat of Turner's car, and he handed her the keys.

"Nice and slow, no heroics, and maybe you'll get out of this alive." He eyed her head. "With a few pieces of your lovely red hair as a memento of this special occasion."

Taking a deep, cleansing breath, she debated on shape-shifting right there and then. The proximity of the needle to her throat, however, gave her pause. Human or wolf, that stuff would kill her—and it would be an agonizing death. Putting the car into drive, she said, "Where to?"

"Ah, I see you've decided to live—for now." He played with a lock of her hair, and she held her breath. He plucked out her earbud, reached around and grabbed the other one. "You won't need these—you'll make plenty of your own music soon." He pointed to a road leading to nowhere that she knew. "Go that way. I've got a place in mind, one where no one will possibly find us."

Keep him talking. Play to his ego and play for time. Please, God, let Jacob find me.

"Since we've got a little time to kill, I'd like to ask

you a few questions. Is that okay?"

He sat back in his seat, the syringe at the ready. "Try me."

"Okay." *Prick his pride.* "In addition to your father, we figure you've killed three women—"

He barked out a laugh. "Oh, my dear little girl, how you've underestimated me."

She feigned amazement. "There are more?"

"The ones you found are the ones I wanted you to find. I do so enjoy the media coverage." He licked his lips. "Delicious to see everyone so confused and lost. You guys couldn't find your ass with two hands."

"Hmm." She shook her head. "Color me skeptical. I'm going to have to be convinced."

"Okay, this is for your edification—and the truth may not set you free, my dear."

She gave a shaky laugh. "I had a feeling I might not get out of this alive, so please, humor me."

"Since you put it that way," he chuckled. "Listen and learn. Did you know grocery stores are the best hunting grounds? Women aren't paying attention to their surroundings. They're busy trying to put their bags into the car and go home." He flicked her hair. "Like the first one, back in June, at Cheap Eats. She was so easy. I gave her my best smile and she melted, of course. Women do find me irresistible."

"I can see that," Zena said. In a Charles Manson, crazy eyes kind of way. "Kind of like Ted Bundy."

"You know your serial killers."

"I'm sure you're better versed than me." *Play to his narcissism.* "Do you have any favorites?"

"Funny you should ask." He smiled. "I think the Casanova Killer's looks were overrated. I'm a hundred times better looking than him, and I beat his numbers."

"Over twenty? It took him decades to rack those numbers up. You haven't been killing that long, have you?"

"How would you know, you stupid bitch?"

"You're so young—"

"Yes, I am. You've got that right, at least." Mollified, he added, "I was always an overachiever. My goal is to exceed Doctor Death's record."

"The British guy who poisoned all those old ladies? How many?"

"Over two-hundred." He nodded. "And they all re-did their wills and signed their estates over to him, too. He had a good gig going, but he got greedy and stupid. The funeral director noticed all his patients were getting cremated."

She nodded agreement. "That is quite a blunder."

"I learn from other's mistakes—that's what makes me unstoppable."

She wanted to smack her forehead. The guy's ego was his undoing. "Who was next? Around here, I mean."

"Coral Little Bear. I saw her for migraines at the clinic. She even let me do a scalp biopsy. Do you believe that?" He snickered. "I took a little more than one would need for that, but she didn't know."

Eddy's mother.

"I'm confused. Her son found her alone in their backyard."

He sighed as if working with a sluggish student. "I gave her some lovely headache medicine, like the kind you can buy in any drug store. However, my packets were enhanced with my special mixture."

"Strychnine and brucine."

"Now you're catching on. Good girl." He patted her hand and waved the syringe toward a cut off into a rundown section of housing. "Turn here."

She complied. "The next victim?"

"Please. I hate that word. You make these women sound so helpless." His voice grew hard. "My Indian mother wasn't helpless when she left me alone to be dropkicked into foster homes. She should have taken better care of herself, not die from a frigging heart attack. It was her duty, her obligation to me." Breathing rapidly and erratically, he paused and said, "I'm done playing this game with you. No more true confessions."

She'd hit a nerve. Mommy problems. How could she use that to her advantage?

"You know, heart disease is pretty common among Native Americans. I'm sure she didn't die on purpose."

"Shut up, bitch." He pointed at a boarded-up house covered in graffiti. "Pull in behind that crack house."

"Meth."

"What?"

"The drug. Meth is the big issue out here."

"Dammit, would you shut up? You're not smarter than me, so give up." He yanked her arm and put the needle by her nose. "One more word and you will die badly."

She nodded, knowing one more push would put him over the edge. She had to bide her time, wait for the right moment.

"Get out." He snatched the keys out of the ignition. "Don't even think of running. I'm in top physical condition and I can run you down like a wolf on a deer."

A giggle caught in her throat, and she pretended to cry.

"Yeah, now you're getting the picture." He grabbed her arm and led her to a door hanging on one hinge. He pushed the door with his foot. "Get in there."

Shoving the cracked, weather-beaten wood aside, she slid into the room and surveyed the space. Definite meth lab potential. All that was missing were the cooks and the ingredients. She needed to talk to Jacob about the dangers of abandoned housing. If she got out of here alive.

"Stand over there." He waved at a nearby wall. "And take off your clothes."

She raised her eyebrows.

"I'm not planning to rape you." He paused. "I'm making sure you're not hiding any weapons. Besides you won't get far naked if you try to make a run for it in this weather."

Zena stripped down, carefully folding her jeans to hide the presence of her phone, and praying it was still in range of a cell tower. Shivering, she covered her breasts and her pubic area.

"Turn around, put your hands on the wall, and spread your legs."

As she complied his footsteps came closer, and a hand ran down her back and cupped a buttock. "Nice ass," he breathed into her ear. "I might have to break my rules and sample the wares."

A car door slammed outside, and the roving hand stopped. "Who the hell is that?"

Taking advantage of the distraction, she raced into an adjacent room and slammed the rickety door. As he pounded on the paper-thin wood, she began to shift, urging her body to move faster in the small space between the commode and sink.

"Come out here now, you stupid bitch. No one is going to save you."

A low growl emerged from her throat. Her vision sharpened, as did her nails as they turned into long claws. Licking her chops, she flicked her tail, and threw herself at the door.

****

Grateful to Bronco for switching seats and taking the wheel of the car when they turned down the broken concrete road, Jacob was in wolf form when they arrived at the broken-down house. The former ATF agent stopped the car, ran around, and opened the door for him. Nose to the ground Jacob trotted to the house and stopped. Zena was in there, and the killer was screaming at her.

No time to waste.

Lifting his nose in the air, he pointed at the shaky door, and Bronco held it aside. The room was empty, save for a pile of denim. He caught Zena's scent—fear, mixed with anger, and something else. Hope?

Slinking around the corner, he watched the madman kicking at the door, the loaded syringe still in his hand. The door exploded, sending ragged pieces of wood out onto the dirty floor. A beautiful red wolf leaped out of the opening—snarling. Seizing the moment, Jacob jumped at Turner and knocked the syringe out of his hand, sending it skittering across the cluttered floor.

Whirling on him, Turner screamed, "What the hell is going on?"

Zena latched onto his leg and chomped down.

Turner shrieked in pain and crumpled to the floor.

Jacob swept his claws across his face, giving him a set of wounds that would match his uncle's when they healed.

Blood ran into Turner's eyes as he screamed in pain and shouted, "Who are you? What are you?"

Gun in hand, Bronco stepped into the room, and nodded at Jacob. "I've got you covered, my friend."

Zena growled.

"It's okay," the big man said. "It's over. You're safe now."

She dropped the killer's leg, and he curled into a ball, whimpering, and sniveling. She flicked her tail and bared her teeth at him.

Not such a big man now, are you, without your poison and your scalpel?

Jacob chuffed. *You got that right.*

"Assume the position," Bronco shouted at Turner. "Face on the ground, hands behind your back."

Still whining, the man cried, "I have rights. You're supposed to read me my rights. I'm going to sue your ass."

"Miranda." Bronco bent down and pulled the white plastic zip tie snug. "Miranda, Miranda."

"I'm a physician. My hands are worth millions. Take that off me."

"You can wriggle your fingers, doc, you'll be fine," Bronco said. He rolled Turner over, and then pulled him to his feet. "We're going to park you right up against this wall for the time being."

Looks like Bronco's got him under control. I'm going to get dressed. Zena's words floated into his mind. She grabbed her clothes with her teeth and trotted into the bathroom, while Jacob kept a watchful gaze on Turner. His bright blue eyes darted back and forth, like a wild animal seeking an exit and finding none.

As soon as Zena returned to the main room, wearing her boots and ready to kick ass, Jacob trotted out to the cruiser to shift back to human form and hurried to get dressed in his uniform. Wouldn't do to be caught out here naked. As he pulled on his windbreaker, someone screamed.

Racing back into the hovel, he searched for Zena and Bronco, who were both alive and well. Turner, on the other hand, foamed at the mouth, his body twisting, and writhing.

"What the hell happened?" Jacob shouted.

"Looks like he could do more than wriggle his fingers," Bronco said and rolled the still twitching man over.

Grasped in his contorted hand was the syringe—with the needle buried in his back.

Chapter Twenty-Three

Crow Reservation ~*~ Crow Agency, Montana

The CSI team worked the abandoned house and Turner's car, while Zena briefed the Chief of the Montana FBI Office, and Jacob spoke to his team by phone off to the side.

Joe walked out behind the gurney with the black body bag and stopped to congratulate Zena. "You got the son of a bitch."

Zena shook her head. "DNA tied him to one murder—not the others. Plus, we don't know if he killed himself intentionally or by accident. I'd like more hard evidence he's the serial killer."

"Your wish may be granted," Jacob said with a huge grin. "The joint team discovered a giant gun safe in his closet."

"Didn't find any firearms on him," Zena mused. "Trophy case?"

"Could be." Jacob nodded at the FBI boss. "Can we go now? I'd like to be at the creep's apartment when they open that sucker."

"Could take a while. I worked this one case—a savings and loan crook stole over one hundred and twenty million from old people, a real lowlife, you know? The scum ball had a *huge* concrete encased safe in his master bedroom. Looked like he was ready for

Armageddon. We had to drill the safe—took over two days because the frigging power kept going out. When we got in, nothing but dust." He snorted. "This was *after* we dug up the sonuvabitch's two-acre property for weeks looking for cash and came up empty. Talk about a letdown."

"Let's hope this guy doesn't have Al Capone's Safe Syndrome, too." Zena snorted. "If he's like most serial killers, he would have wanted mementoes to relive the murders and fantasize about them."

"Hey, before you go," the Montana FBI Chief asked, "How did Jacob and Bronco find you?"

Crap. I can't tell him Jacob tracked me by scent alone. Think fast.

"My wireless earbuds were decoys," she lied.

"When he flicked them out while I was driving, he didn't find the tiny real ones underneath those."

"Smart move." He nodded. "Make sure you put that in your report. Good to know for other agents."

"Yes, sir, will do."

Bronco caught her gaze, nodded, and gave her a two fingered salute.

Phew. She was right not to blow his cover.

Jacob slapped her on the back. "That's our girl, smart and tough."

"Did you call me a girl?"

He put his hands up. "Sorry. Special Agent Adalwolf."

She grinned. "That's better. Let's get moving."

A short while later, they dropped Bronco off at his house. He climbed out of the SUV and stuck his head through Zena's window. "That was fun. Please keep me in mind for your next take down."

Standing in the door, Emma called out, "Did you get the killer?"

"We think we did," Zena responded. "You'll know pretty soon if he's our guy."

"Good." Emma shuddered. "It could have been me. I'm his type. God only knows, I could have run into him anywhere."

Zena waved at the handsome couple and headed to the Doctor's apartment. "Talk to you later." She turned to Jacob. "I like them. Maybe we could do dinner with them?"

"Making friends and settling in already, I see." He smirked. "Makes my heart go pit-a-pat."

"You still owe me a game of explorer," she said and grabbed his thigh. "The unknown country awaits me."

He reached for her, pulled her close, and kissed the top of her head. "Grab a little higher and we can pull over and play cowgirl and Indian right here."

"Only if we can do it in the cage," she laughed. "Cops and robbers."

He turned into the parking lot and grinned. "I see boundless opportunities for sex games in our future."

Zena pulled on a pair of black nitrile gloves and wriggled her fingers at him. "Wanna play doctor?"

He grimaced. "Not so sure about that one."

"Too soon?" She quirked an eyebrow. "Give it some time."

A uniformed tribal officer guarding the scene greeted them with a nod as they arrived. "Glad to see you're both safe."

Carts of CSI equipment sat inside the open apartment door. Cabinets and drawers dangled open, sofa cushions lay on the floor, and detritus from a hurried search was strewn everywhere.

"What cleaning company fixes this mess when we're done?" She laughed. "I'm pretty messy, I think I need them for my place."

A shout went up in the next room.

"Action's in the bedroom." Jacob hustled ahead. "What's up?"

An FBI agent gave the thumbs up. "I spoke with the local sports equipment retailer who sold this sucker to our guy. The manager remembered him because he paid cash and didn't seem like a gun enthusiast, kept remarking on the lining of the safe."

"Wow, that's not creepy, at all." Zena stuck her tongue out. "Can they give us the combination?"

"Checking their files as we speak. It's a big chain and they have computer records. Even if he gave them a phony name, they could narrow it down. They *delivered* it to him."

"Oh, my," Zena said. "Looks like he broke rule number one."

Jacob quirked a brow at her. "And that would be?"

"Don't shit where you eat." She tapped the safe. "He wanted the mementoes close by so he could revel in them. Keeping this type of evidence in his house? That's stupid crook material."

The agent on the phone with the store manager gave Jacob a thumb up. "Thank you, sir, yes, please text it to me at this number. We appreciate it."

Her entire body tingled with anticipation, and the room filled with the rest of the crew's tense enthusiasm. The agent turned the knob right three times, then left two times, and right one time, then pushed a rod on the large three-pronged wheel. Nothing happened.

A collective sigh of disappointment filled the small space.

"I must have overshot the number by a hair. Hold on." He tried again, then again. On the third attempt, the wheel turned, and the door swung open.

A blanket of silence fell over the previously excited crowd.

The agent exhaled, "Sweet Mother of God."

Carefully pinned to the soft velvet lining of the gun safe were rows of scalps, each numbered and dated, like specimens in a museum minus names. A Styrofoam head sat on a large shelf on the right side of the safe with a full head of long, black hair, simply numbered *Fifty* with the date of the kill.

Mary Longbow. I'd bet my paycheck on it.

A CSI tech ran to the bathroom, the sounds of retching following him. Zena hoped it wasn't contagious. She clapped her hands and it sounded like thunder in the tiny room.

"You know the drill, folks. Photos, photos, photos, photos, at every conceivable angle. Fingerprints—don't assume he was a loner. He might have had an accomplice. We get this party started and we do this by the book—right Jacob?" She threw him a look that said *help me out here* and wondered if his gag reflex had been about to kick in, too.

"Yes, we do," he agreed. "You know the rules. When the unsub is non-Native, the FBI is in charge. *Everything* is to be done to FBI specs."

Almost in unison, the techs yelled, "Got it!"

"You are team awesome," she enthused. "Thank you for getting us this far. We want to make sure this is our one and only killer, and that we don't have a second one waiting to pick up where he left off."

"That would be unusual, wouldn't it, a killing couple?" Jacob asked.

"Rare, but not unheard of." She shrugged. "The Lonely Hearts Killers were a husband and wife dyad. They put ads in the newspapers to lure victims. A number of males have been known to bond through killings, sort of a pervert's friend to lovers romance trope, or lovers gifting each other with victims to kill. I'm being cautious."

He shuddered. "Okay, you've convinced me."

An hour later the FBI and Tribal CSI agreed they had all the photos and fingerprints they needed from the safe. One of the techs handed a three-ring binder to Zena. "This was way back in the bottom, under a plastic box of hair products. Knew you'd want to see it."

She nodded. "Thanks—I think?" Jacob looked over her shoulder, which wasn't that hard with their height differences. "Ready to take a look into the mind of a serial killer?"

"The suspense is *killing* me."

She groaned. "Puns, so soon?"

"You need to meet more of my teasing cousins. They're punnier than I am."

Shaking her head, she moved to the kitchen counter, pulled up a stool, patted the one next to her for Jacob to take a seat, and opened the notebook with care.

Two section-dividers were labeled *Childhood* and *Experiments*. Zena flipped the first divider back and swallowed hard. Placed in the center of a plastic page protector was a small newspaper with a black border.

DEATH NOTICE: On Monday, January 15, 1996,

Rose Turner, died of natural causes. Her remains have been interred pursuant to the Indigent Person laws of the State of Connecticut. Surviving relatives should contact the Department of Social Services for further information.

"The same year my father died," Jacob breathed.

Small sticky notes festooned the border of the article, their cheerful colors contrasting with slashes of hateful words—BITCH, MOMMY DEAREST, MONSTER, YOU LEFT ME, repeated over and over.

"Well, that explains his preference for killing around the middle of the month—at least initially. He escalated recently—my guess, he knew he was going to get caught and wanted to get all the fun in he could."

"No headshot with the death notice," Jacob observed.

"Costs money," she responded dryly and flipped the page. A beautiful woman with long black hair held a dark-haired infant on her lap and a handsome man with blond hair and a towheaded toddler at his knee smiled up at her.

"Mama, Daddy, and babies make—four?" Jacob wondered. "I think we've accounted for three. Where's the other kid?"

She turned the page and whispered, "I think we found her."

The headline of a yellowed newspaper clipping screamed *Local Girl Murdered.* Beneath the article a neon orange sticky note proclaimed, NUMBER ONE— MY SISTER! A page of handwritten notes detailed how he had killed her and what he did wrong—with a grade of *F* and notes to himself on how to improve his technique.

Jacob grunted. "Sick bastard."

A letter with spidery handwriting followed the article, along with a page of test results from a DNA test with a popular genealogy website.

Stomach roiling, Zena read the letter from Alfred Gunter Turner to his one and only son. Vision blurry, she willed herself not to cry. *This is evidence. Control your emotions.*

Department of Social Services documents followed, all with Brett Turner's name on it, the final one releasing him from the foster care system when he turned age eighteen. Flipping through the rest of the pages, one after another the numbered—but never named—victims appeared in sequence, all with the same types of careful analyses, all with grades, feedback on how to progress, and pats on his own back—"Good job!" "Awesome work!" "Nicely done!". Unable to read any more of his congratulatory notes to himself, Zena snapped the notebook shut. "Guess grades in school were the only positive validations he had as a foster child."

"Not feeling sorry for a psychopath," Jacob said in a hard voice.

"He wasn't only compulsive about killing, he was obsessed with recording and assessing his performance with each one. Great bedtime reading for him, lots of material for his fantasies, along with the trophies. The only good thing about this is we will be able to notify the families who did this to their loved ones. Unless the CSI crew turns up additional evidence to the contrary, I think we can say he acted alone."

"The mayor will be happy to hear the news."

"I'm going to call the Montana FBI Chief on his

cell phone. He'll want to hear this ASAP. I'll let him give the mayor the news."

"Sucking up to the boss already, I see," he said with a grin.

She shrugged. "Following protocol."

He whispered, "What about us?"

Heat rising in her face, she responded, "How about a test run—tonight?"

Epilogue

Crow Reservation ~*~ Crow Agency, Montana

After tucking Eddy into bed, Esther wiped the kitchen counter with long, sweeping curves, taking pleasure in the surface going from dirty to clean. Housekeeping, most people's nemesis, was the time she called her *moving meditation.* Her mind stilled, her breath slowed, and she focused only on the spots and streaks before her. *Right, left, right, left—*

Jessie chuffed, and she looked up, expecting Jacob to come through the door. Instead, her husband strode toward her, no longer covered in blood, and he was smiling. He took her into his arms and twirled her around in a familiar dance routine they'd practiced in the kitchen over two decades ago. Laughing, she stopped, reached out to touch his cheek—and grabbed at emptiness, only air.

"Too good to be true," she whispered. "My imagination is working overtime."

"Hello, Esther." His voice reverberated throughout her body.

Her hand flew to her mouth. "You're here, not a spirit in my head?"

"Yes, but it's time for me to go to the next campground," he said. "The stone holding me here is gone. My murderer is caught, as is the other one."

She gasped. "They caught the serial killer?"

He nodded. "Please don't cry, my love."

She brushed tears off her cheek. "Losing you once was bad enough. Now I lose you again? Can't you stay—like other spirits do?"

"I'm tired and I need to rest." He heaved a great sigh. "It's been almost thirty years since I've been able to sleep."

"I'm sorry," she breathed. "I was being selfish. I had no idea how much energy it took for you to be with me. Is that why you couldn't speak to me before?"

He nodded. "The murders of our Crow women bled my spirit—and continues to bleed all our tribes. I can do no more."

"One last dance?" she begged. "I promise to release you and send you on with my love and prayers."

He held his arms out, and they waltzed.

****

Two months after wrapping up the biggest case in her young career, Zena logged into her personal email account. A bold subject line screamed at her. *New discoveries for Zena Adalwolf!* Her pulse sped up and her mouth went dry. *Is this the day I find my biological family?*

The fact that Turner's father had been able to find him through a genealogical website had plucked at her brain so hard, she had broken down and signed up for one of the numerous tests available commercially. Even as she had spit into that stupid plastic test tube, she'd called herself a fool. A gimmick to get your money, her rational side chided. But what if I do have relatives out there—and they're waiting to meet me, her hopeful side threw back. This is an opportunity to either open a door to new relatives, or firmly close it behind her. Either way, she *had* to know.

She opened the email. *You've got DNA connections! Take a look at your results!* Zena clicked the link—and whooped. Cousins! She had cousins and uncles and aunts and—she scrolled back up. *How could that be?*

Jacob appeared in the door of her home office wearing only a towel around his waist. "You okay, babe?"

"As much as you are *terribly* distracting with those hunky six-pack abs—" She leaped up from the chair, almost dropping her own terrycloth wrap, and gave him a passionate kiss. "I've got some amazing news to share with you." She pointed at the monitor, and he bent down to use the mouse. The temptation to grab his ass nearly overwhelmed her, but if she did that, they'd never get to his mother's house in time for Sabbath dinner.

"What am I looking at?" He frowned. "Whose DNA is this?"

"Mine." She shrugged. "I didn't tell you because I wasn't sure what would happen. Turns out, I have a whole lot of relatives, dozens of cousins—and if this test is correct, a sister."

"Another one of you?" He shook his head. "I'm not sure the world is ready for that dynamic duo."

She laughed—and then grew somber. "What do I say to my adoptive parents? I owe them so much. They saved my life, gave me the best world they could. I don't want them to think I'm ungrateful."

Jacob pulled her into a hug and kissed the top of her head. "No one would ever begrudge you wanting to find out what happened that day. Trust me, I know how this has been eating at you."

She snuggled into his hard chest and inhaled his woodsy scent. *Damn, she loved this man.* "Jacob?"

He rubbed her back and ran his hand down to her buttocks. "Yeah?"

"How much time do we have before we need to be at your mother's?"

He swept her off her feet and strode toward the bedroom, all the while nuzzling at the sensitive crook of her neck. "Time enough."

****

"Eddy, are you almost ready?" Esther shook her head. *That boy.* When it came to getting cleaned up, a sloth would beat him.

He walked into the kitchen wearing his new plaid shirt, jeans, and cowboy boots. "I am not a sloth." He grinned. "I'm a snail."

"Of course, silly me."

"Where is everyone?" He grabbed a chunk of challah before Esther could pull the plate away from him.

"Wait for the blessings," she chided.

"But I'm hungry," he protested.

Jessie chuffed and wagged her tail.

"Don't encourage him," she said to the dog.

The door opened and her son and Zena walked in.

"Jacob, Zena, so glad you're here. Did you happen to see Wanda and Tommy?"

Jacob jerked his thumb. "Right behind us."

Struggling to get through the door with a baby carrier, diaper bag, and all the accoutrements of an infant, Tommy gasped, "Present and accounted for."

Wanda brought up the rear with a platter covered with pastries and fruit. "Where do I put this?"

Esther pointed at a space on the counter. "Move those bowls to the side."

Jacob introduced Zena to Wanda. "Isn't there some law of physics that says it's dangerous to have more than one redhead in the room at a time?"

Zena punched him in the arm. "Only if you keep talking that way."

"Mom, what happened to that other doctor at the clinic? The one you called the Teddy Bear."

Esther stirred the matzah ball soup and turned the burner down. "Well, Robert's husband left him. Poor guy got a Dear John letter around the same time Brett Turner's father showed up at the clinic." She shook her head. "He was devastated. But thanks to Stephanie, she introduced him to a new beau, an eco-tour guide. Robert calls him Mr. Rugged and says it was love at first sign. Looks like the Teddy Bear is going to stay around for a while."

Someone knocked at the door, and the conversation stopped. Heat rushed up her neck, and her heart did a little tumble and dance with her stomach.

Jacob frowned, "Who could that be? Isn't everyone here?"

Eddy opened his mouth, and she silenced him with a glare and beamed a warning. *Not a word.*

She smoothed her apron, flicked her hair off her face, and opened the door. "Hal," she breathed, "so glad you could join us."

He bent down and planted a kiss on her lips. "Me, too."

She turned to the group and burst out laughing.

"Oh, my stars, if you could see yourselves right now. You look like a school of guppies!"

The silence melted into greetings and a hub bub of happy noise, music to her ears.

She placed the candles in the holder and began the Sabbath prayers. *"Baruch atah Adonai Eloheinu..."* At the end, everyone said "Amen."

"Take a seat wherever you like," she ordered, "but do take a seat—all except Jacob. I need his help."

He strode to the stove, bent his head to his mother's, and began to fill the bowls. "Now?"

"Hmm, no, let's do the other thing first, if you don't mind? A double *chai*?"

He nodded. "How many balls does everyone want? One or two?"

Eddy shouted, "Two, because—"

"You're always hungry," the family chimed in unison.

"Eddy," Esther said as she passed the challah to him. "Remember what we talked about?"

He nodded and gave her a lop-sided grin. "Yup."

"Wanda and Tommy have something to ask you." She pointed a soup spoon at the couple.

Wanda flushed and cleared her throat. "First of all, Eddy, I want to apologize to you. After I had the baby, I had post-partum depression, and I wasn't very nice to you." Tommy squeezed her hand. "I got treatment, and I can tell you I'm not that awful person anymore."

Eddy cocked his head and Esther knew he was listening to Wanda's thoughts. *Smart boy.*

He nodded. "I understand. It's hard having a baby. They cry a lot and don't sleep."

"Do you forgive me? I promise to be nicer to you,

to everyone now."

"I know you will." He laughed and covered his mouth—undoubtedly, about to reveal something embarrassing.

"Eddy," Tommy began, "the owner of the grocery store decided to drop the charges against you."

"Yes!" He clapped his hands. "I didn't want to go to the slammer like my dad."

"You weren't going to jail," Tommy laughed. "Maybe some community service. Not that it would have been a *bad* thing for you."

"Yeah." Eddy lowered his eyes, his cheeks reddening.

"Have you considered our offer?" Tommy asked. "Would you be willing to try to live with us again?"

Esther's heart twisted a little in her chest, and her vision blurred. She gripped his hand in hers. "You can always come visit me. You know this is your home, too."

"Well," Eddy glanced between Esther and Tommy. "I'll give it a try—as long as I get to bring my comic books."

"Hey," Jacob protested. "Those are mine."

Eddy grinned. "I know. I'm borrowing them."

A while later, with dinner over and the dessert platter on the table, everyone groaned and complained about how stuffed they were—even Eddy.

"Now?" Jacob whispered to Esther as he helped to clear the dishes.

She glanced at the table. Wanda and Zena played with the baby and chatted. She nodded and said in a soft voice, "Go for it."

Jacob went to Zena's side and got down to one

knee.

"What's wrong?" Zena exclaimed. "Did you drop something?"

Jacob pulled a black velvet box from behind his back and snapped it open. "Zena Adalwolf, will you marry me?"

Esther held her breath.

Zena grabbed his head and pulled him in for a kiss.

When they came up for air, Jacob said, "Is that a yes?"

"Yes, yes, a thousand times, yes!"

The kitchen erupted in cheers, clapping, and mazel tovs—even the baby joined in with a howl.

Esther placed her hand on her heart and tears spilled down her cheeks. Her mind went to Joseph, and how proud he would be of their son. She wished he could be there right now to see this moment. A cool breeze caressed her neck, carrying the words, "I am with you, always and forever."

Author's Note

Anyone who has read my previous novels knows that I conduct extensive research and obtain feedback from subject matter experts and readers with diverse backgrounds before I submit a story for consideration for publication. I would be remiss if I did not thank my readers here, starting with my ever-patient husband, Dale Buchbinder, who read every single draft of the story. My deep gratitude goes to the following people for their expertise and feedback: Joshua and Elyse Buchbinder, Toni Chiazza DiBlasi, Kathi Goldwyn, Susan Hutchinson, Deborah Leather, John Tobin, Nellie Mercer, Sharon Saracino, Sonia Vitale-Richardson, and Susan Willis. Big hugs to my brilliant editor and book mid-wife, Amanda Barnett, who assists with the birth of my book babies.

In this book, I have used the words "Indian" and "Native" interchangeably. I gave this great consideration and chose to do this after researching standard nomenclature among scholarly publications and current Native news outlets, such as Indian Country Today. The term "Indian Country" refers to reservations and adjacent areas around reservations and land allotments, all of which are under the supervision of the federal government. The U.S. Congress determines what is or is not a tribe and as of this writing, there are 574 federally recognized tribes. The size of reservations range from small, such as the federally recognized Augustine Band of Cahuilla Indians on 20 acres in southern California with eight enrolled members as of 2002, and the Navajo Nation with over 27,000 square miles, crossing four states (aka, Four Corners, Utah, Colorado, Arizona, and New Mexico), with almost 400,000 members.

The recognition of the epidemic of Missing and Murdered Indigenous Women (MMIW) by politicians and judicial policy makers is long overdue. The 2018 Urban Indian Health Institute's report, Missing and Murdered Indigenous Women & Girls (MMIWG), indicates that in 2016, "5,712 cases of MMIWG were reported, but only 116 of them were logged into the Department of Justice's missing persons database" (p. 2). Additionally, the Coalition to Stop Violence Against Native Women reports, "4 out of 5 of our Native women are affected by violence" and "American Indians face murder rates that are more than 10 times the national average" (2019, para. 1). Collecting, organizing, and disseminating the data through national crime databases has been a major problem. On and off reservation, many Native families have suffered from the loss or murder of a loved one—on some reservations, everyone has lost a member of their family or a friend. It is only due to the diligence and passion of Native American epidemiologists, advocates, and allies that this discrepancy between what is known and what is recorded has come to light in recent years.

Colonization, institutionalized racism, and misogyny all contribute to the MMIW epidemic, but these elements don't fully explain it. Another large part of this underrecognized epidemic involves the existence of complicated laws that make it difficult for local, state, federal, and tribal jurisdictions to work together to address common issues. I highly recommend Stephen L. Pevar's *The Rights of Indians and Tribes,* 4th edition which puts all these laws in a historical perspective and lays out issues associated with them. The Supreme Court of the United States (SCOTUS) 1978 decision in the Oliphant v. Suquamish Indian Tribe has had the greatest impact on the MMIW epidemic. This decision "held that Indian tribes may not prosecute non-Indians without the express consent of Congress, and Congress has not consented to this type of tribal jurisdiction" (Pevar, 2012, p. 140). Per Pevar, "...70 percent of violent crimes committed on reservations are committed by non-Indians (60 percent by whites, and 10 percent by other racial groups)", (p. 132). In areas of oil and gas extraction, with a large influx of male workers, incidents of rape, abduction, and murder increase exponentially (Mary Kathryn Nagle, on Democracy Now, October 10, 2019). The SCOTUS decision of 1978 gives non-Native violent offenders a get out of jail free card because they know they cannot be arrested by tribal authorities, let alone prosecuted. Tribal authorities must depend on the state and federal authorities to prosecute these criminals—and they haven't been doing a good job.

In November 2019, the glacial speed of the federal government to the MMIW epidemic picked up, in large part in response to advocacy efforts and public outcry. The Department of Justice announced a long overdue creation of the Missing and Murdered Indigenous Persons (MMIP) Initiative. This project will create positions in order to coordinate any approach between state, local, federal, and tribal law enforcement efforts. There will be "MMIP coordinators, specialized FBI rapid deployment teams, and comprehensive data analysis" along with "coordination between 50 US Attorneys" (DOJ, 2019, paras. 5-8). The Senate Indian

Affairs Committee moved Savanna's Act and the Not Invisible Law out of committee to the Senate floor. Finally, the President signed an Executive Order on MMIW in late November 2019, recognizing the MMIW epidemic and establishing a Task Force on Missing and Murdered American Indians and Alaska Natives (Task Force) and delineating the membership, mission, and powers of the taskforce. To commemorate this epidemic, May 5 was designated National Day of Awareness for Missing and Murdered Native Women and Girls (MMIWG).

The Indian Child Welfare Act (ICWA) was enacted in 1978 after a Congressional investigation "revealed that between 25 and 35 percent of Indian children had been removed from their families" by the state and placed in foster homes—the majority (85 percent) in non-Indian homes (Pevar, 2012, p. 292). To put this in perspective, imagine the outcry if one in four children in your community was taken away and placed with strangers from a different culture, speaking a different language. Through ICWA, the tribes now control all placements of children who are wards of the tribal court. Placements are, in order of preference, immediate relatives, extended family members, foster care among members of the tribe. Tribal control of their children's welfare is critical to maintaining community, language, and culture. An entire generation of tribal members was lost through the forced relocation of Indian children to Residential Schools. The US held the children captive to force Native Americans to give their lands up. Once there, the children were not permitted to speak their own language or participate in any cultural rituals or events. Those who broke the rules were often physically disciplined, many dying of tuberculosis and other diseases in these strange places. Only recently have the remains of some of children been returned to their tribes (Estes, 2019; History.com, 2018).

The quality of reservation life varies from place to place and tribe to tribe. It is a myth that all reservations have casinos and all Native Americans are wealthy. In fact, less than half (42%) of the federally recognized tribes have casinos, and few are rich from gambling (Robertson, 2017). One-quarter of all Native Americans live below the poverty line. Some reservations, like Pine Ridge Reservation, lack basic utilities such as clean water and electricity. Only 14 percent of all Native Americans graduate from a university or college (American Indian College Fund, 2019). The US Congress is responsible for Native American welfare, and you can do something about these disparities by writing and calling your Representatives and Senators to demand they do better by Native Americans. In addition, there are many charities that would welcome your donations. As always, check to see they are reputable before donating. Among my favorites are the American Indian College Fund, Northern Plains Reservation Aid, Native American Rights Fund (NARF), Running Strong for Indian Youth, and Vision Maker Media, which creates Native stories for public broadcasting.

Red wolves, which are a different species from the gray wolf, are facing extinction. They are not related to coyotes but are true wolves. They are smaller than gray wolves and hunt small mammals. As of this writing "about 40 red wolves roam their native habitats in eastern North Carolina as a non-essential, experimental population (NEP), and more than 200 red wolves are maintained in captive breeding facilities throughout the US" (US Fish & Wildlife Service, 2019). As the wolves are bred and the pups mature, they are released back into the wild where they belong. Sometimes mistaken for coyotes or gray wolves, these beautiful creatures are still threatened by hunters. If you are interested in helping to protect red wolves, there are not-for-profit centers around the country that would welcome your help.

I hope you enjoy this story. If you are interested in sources I used to research this novel in addition to those cited here, I would be happy to share my list with you. Just email me at:

sharonbellbuchbinder@gmail.com

Happy reading!
Sharon Buchbinder

American Indian College Fund. (2019). Meet our team. Retrieved from:
https://collegefund.org/about-us/team/

Coalition to Stop Violence Against Native Women (CSVANW). (2019). MMIW Retrieved from:
https://www.csvanw.org/mmiw/

Department of Justice (DOJ). (2019, November). Attorney General launches national strategy to address Missing and Murdered Indigenous Persons. Retrieved from:
https://www.justice.gov/usao-mn/pr/attorney-general-launches-national-strategy-address-missing-and-murdered-indigenous

Democracy Now. (2019, October 10). Justice for Kaysera: Native teen's mysterious death highlights epidemic of murdered Indigenous women. Retrieved from:
https://www.democracynow.org/2019/10/10/kaysera_ stops_pretty_places_family_justice

Estes, N. (2019, October 14). The U.S. stole generations of Indigenous children to open the West. Retrieved from:
https://www.hcn.org/issues/51.17/indigenous-affairs-the-us-stole-generations-of-indigenous-children-to-open-the-west

Indian Country Today:
https://newsmaven.io/indiancountrytoday/

Little, B. (2018, November 1). Government boarding schools once separated Native American children from families. Retrieved from:
https://www.history.com/news/government-boarding-schools-separated-native-american-children-families

National Indigenous Women's Resource Center (NIWRC). (2019). Retrieved from:
https://www.niwrc.org/resources/special-collection-missing-murdered-indigenous-women-girls

Native American Aid (NAA). (2015). Living conditions. Retrieved from:
http://www.nativepartnership.org/site/PageServer?page name=naa_livingconditions

Native News Online Staff. (2020, May 5). May 5 is

National Day of Awareness for Missing and Murdered Native Women and Girls. Retrieved from: https://nativenewsonline.net/currents/may-5-is-national-day-of-awareness-for-missing-and-murdered-native-women-and-girls

Not Invisible Law: https://www.congress.gov/bill/116th-congress/senate-bill/982/text

Pevar. S.L. (2012). The rights of Indians and tribes, 4th edition. New York, NY: Oxford University Press.

Robertson, D.L. (2017). The myth of Indian casino riches. Retrieved from: https://newsmaven.io/indiancountrytoday/archive/the-myth-of-indian-casino-riches-3H8eP-wHX0Wz0H4WnQjwjA

Savanna's Act: https://www.congress.gov/bill/116th-congress/senate-bill/227/text

The White House. (2019). Executive order on establishing the Task Force on Missing and Murdered American Indians and Alaska Natives. Retrieved from: https://www.whitehouse.gov/presidential-actions/executive-order-establishing-task-force-missing-murdered-american-indians-alaska-natives/

US Fish & Wildlife Service. (2017). Retrieved from: https://www.fws.gov/southeast/wildlife/mammals/red-wolf/

A word about the author…

Amazon best-selling author Sharon Buchbinder's broad range of writing includes internationally best-selling textbooks and award-winning novels that tell haunting tales of love, family secrets, forgiveness, extraordinary abilities, truth, justice, and redemption. She believes happily-ever-afters are born through strengths developed in overcoming adversity in fiction and real life.

If you enjoy authors Heather Graham, Christine Feehan, and Nalini Singh, you will probably enjoy Sharon's Western romance ghost stories, woven with supernatural, Native American paranormal suspense elements. Set in small towns in the American West with strong female heroines, sexy male heroes, secret government agencies, undercover agents, shape-shifters, werewolves, weretigers, ghosts, jinnis (genies), telekinesis, teleportation, and remote viewing, these stories will make you wonder about those bumps in the night.

For more information go to:
https://www.sharonbuchbinder.com

Other Titles from Sharon at The Wild Rose Press...

Kiss of the Jinni Hunter Series ~

Kiss of the Silver Wolf
Kiss of the Virgin Queen

~*~

Single Title ~

Obsession
Some Other Child

~*~

The Hotel Labelle Series ~

The Haunting of Hotel Labelle
Legacy of Evil
Eye of the Eagle

Thank you for purchasing
this publication of The Wild Rose Press, Inc.

For questions or more information
contact us at
info@thewildrosepress.com.

The Wild Rose Press, Inc.
www.thewildrosepress.com